A · TREASURY · OF
JEWISH
STORIES

CHOSEN BY
Adèle Geras

ILLUSTRATED BY
Jane Cope

Kingfisher

CONTENTS

KINGFISHER • TREASURIES

Ideal for reading aloud with younger children, or for more experienced readers to enjoy independently, Kingfisher *Treasuries* provide the very best writing for children. Carefully chosen by expert compilers, the content of each book is varied and wide-ranging. There are modern stories and traditional folk tales and fables, stories from a variety of cultures around the world and writing from exciting contemporary authors.

Popular with both children and their parents, books in the *Treasury* series provide a useful introduction to new authors, and encourage children to extend their reading.

01424

KINGFISHER
An imprint of Larousse plc
Elsley House, 24-30 Great Titchfield Street
London W1P 7AD

First published by Kingfisher 1996
2 4 6 8 10 9 7 5 3 1

This selection copyright © Adèle Geras 1996
Illustrations copyright © Jane Cope 1996

The moral right of the authors, editor and illustrator has been asserted.

A CIP catalogue record for this book
is available from the British Library

ISBN 01 85697 475 8

Printed in Great Britain

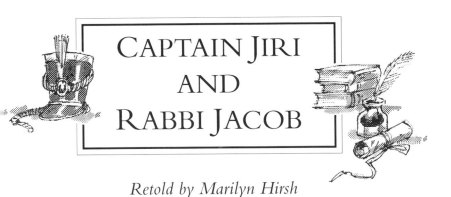

CAPTAIN JIRI
AND
RABBI JACOB

Retold by Marilyn Hirsh

Long ago, in the city of Cracow, there lived an old rabbi named Jacob. He was so good that the neighbours said, "He's an angel from heaven." The children were always creeping up behind him to look for his wings, but they could never find them.

At the same time, in the city of Prague, there lived a brave, strong soldier named Captain Jiri. His job was to guard the main bridge that led into the city. When the good people saw him, they felt safe, but the bad people were afraid and ran away.

Rabbi Jacob's house was filled with old books. The children came to study and learn about the laws of God and man. In a corner, the old men argued about the very same laws. Some discussions went on for days, but everybody loved to argue, so it didn't matter.

For years, Captain Jiri led his men up and down over the bridge. Through snow and sleet and the hottest summer days, he and his soldiers protected the people of Prague. They were always ready to fight, even if it wasn't necessary.

Captain Jiri and his men were all the sons of poor peasants. They could not read or write and only knew how to be good soldiers. At night, when they finished work, they began to drink. After a while, some would fall asleep, and some would fight. Captain Jiri felt there must

be a better way to live, but he didn't know what it was.

Rabbi Jacob had his troubles, too. On the way to and from his house, his students were often chased by bullies from other neighbourhoods. The children were used to studying and didn't know how to protect themselves. Rabbi Jacob worried about the children's safety. He looked through his old books and found answers to many strange and wonderful questions. But he didn't find anything that would help him keep the children safe.

One night, a guardian angel, dressed like Captain Jiri, appeared to Rabbi Jacob. "In the city of Prague, under the main bridge, there is a great treasure," the angel announced. "This treasure is for you." Without realizing that he had visited the wrong person, the angel disappeared.

On the very same night, a guardian angel, dressed like Rabbi Jacob, appeared to Captain Jiri. "In the city of Cracow, in the house of Rabbi Jacob, there is a great treasure," the angel announced. "This treasure is for you." Without realizing that he, too, had visited the wrong person, the angel disappeared.

It is not right to ignore an angel, so early the next morning, Rabbi Jacob set out for Prague. At the same time, Captain Jiri set out for Cracow. The road was filled with knights and ladies, farmers and merchants, jugglers and beggars. The trip was exciting but very long and tiring. Rabbi Jacob had to stop and rest along the way, but Captain Jiri marched steadily on without getting tired. They passed each other on the road without even knowing it.

Rabbi Jacob finally arrived in Prague. He easily found the main bridge, but all that he found under it was water. He noticed the soldiers of Captain Jiri's company. If only my students looked like that, no one would bother them, he thought. After three days of looking under, over, and around the bridge, Rabbi Jacob decided to go home. That was a  funny-looking angel, he thought. It was probably just a dream.

Captain Jiri had a hard time finding Rabbi Jacob's house, but he finally did. He went inside and started looking around. The children and old men were so busy arguing that they didn't even notice him. Captain Jiri was glad to hear the students arguing about ideas instead of fighting and drinking. If only my soldiers could learn to argue like that, he thought. Captain Jiri did not find his treasure and decided to go home. The angel was pretty funny-looking, he thought. It was probably something I ate.

Rabbi Jacob and Captain Jiri both started on the

long road home. But as they were passing one another, they noticed something strange. They stopped and stared at each other.

"You look like an angel," said Captain Jiri.

"Well, so do you," said Rabbi Jacob.

Just then, the guardian angels appeared. "In the city of Prague, under the main bridge, there is a great treasure," announced the angel who looked like Captain Jiri. "This treasure is for you."

"For me?" asked Rabbi Jacob and Captain Jiri together.

"Do not interrupt angels," said the angels.

"In the city of Cracow, in the house of Rabbi Jacob, there is a great treasure," announced the other angel, who looked like Rabbi Jacob. "This treasure is for you."

"For me?" Rabbi Jacob and Captain Jiri cried again.

"We have said all this twice now," declared the guardian angels together and disappeared into a passing cloud.

Rabbi Jacob and Captain Jiri watched them go in amazement and then looked at each other. They began to smile as they realized that even guardian angels can make mistakes. In a moment they said goodbye and hurried to their own homes.

Rabbi Jacob and all his family looked everywhere for the treasure. Finally, in a dark niche high above the fireplace, he found an old bag. When he opened the bag, out came a lot of dust and hundreds of gold coins.

Captain Jiri knew about a big loose stone under the bridge. I'm sure that's the spot for a treasure, he thought. And he was right! As soon as the stone was pulled out, the soldiers could see bright gold coins in a big bag.

Rabbi Jacob remembered the soldiers and how brave they looked. With his treasure, he bought the children uniforms with bright red hats. He hired an old soldier to teach them how to defend themselves. Soon their cheeks turned pink, and their eyes were bright. The next time the bullies came by, the students yelled and made their scariest faces. They chased the bullies out of the neighbourhood, and they did not come back. Rabbi Jacob and the children agreed that it

was healthy to defend themselves, and they should make it part of their studies from then on.

Captain Jiri remembered the books and discussions in Rabbi Jacob's house. He used his treasure to buy books and hired an old scholar to teach the soldiers to read. One soldier learned to write poetry and another to play the lute. One became a fine artist, while another knitted long socks of his own design. One preferred to continue drinking and did so.

Captain Jiri and Rabbi Jacob met every so often to discuss their experiences with angels. Captain Jiri advised Rabbi Jacob on training the children, and Rabbi Jacob brought Captain Jiri some new books to read. They were happy that their guardian angels had made a mistake, or they never would have become friends.

A MENSCH IS SOMEONE SPECIAL

Phyllis Rose Eisenberg

After school on Friday, I go to Grandma Esther's. I am helping her make dinner. She has invited four people: me, my parents, and Mrs Fogelman who lives next door.

I am happy about me and my parents. I am not happy about Mrs Fogelman.

First of all, she tells me what to do. Second, she doesn't care what I think. Third, she doesn't look at me or smile at me. Fourth, she calls me Lees instead of Lisa. I've told Grandma about the Lees part, but not the rest.

"You never had Mrs Fogelman before," I say to Grandma.

"Mr Fogelman is away on business, so it'll be nice for her to be here," says Grandma as she chops the liver. She is the fastest chopper in the world.

Big pieces turn to little pieces right away. "Please hand me the onion, Lisa."

Next to the egg part, which *I* get to do, I like the onion part best. It makes Grandma's eyes water.

"How come you're not crying?" I say as she peels the onion.

"Don't rush me, Bubeleh," says Grandma. (I like her to call me *Bubeleh*. It means "little grand-mother.") "I'll be crying in no time."

"Do you ever cry without onions, Grandma?" I say.

"Sometimes when I think of your Grandpa Nathan," she says.

"Tell me a story about him," I say. Grandma is a very good storyteller.

She wipes her eyes. "He was a real *mensch*," she says sighing.

"What's a mensch, Grandma?"

Grandma puts her hands on my shoulders the way she does when she has something important to tell me. "A mensch, Lisa, is a fine human being. Someone you can count on, no matter what."

While I am wondering if *I'll* ever be a mensch, Grandma opens the refrigerator. "Lisa," she says, "there's only one egg. Please borrow two more from Mrs Fogelman."

I hate going to Mrs Fogelman's. So I say, "I'll go right after you tell about Grandpa Nathan." I'm hoping by then she'll forget and go herself.

"All right," says Grandma. "Once Grandpa Nathan had waited a whole year to see a certain movie. Finally it came to our neighbourhood, but a minute after it started, I broke part of my tooth eating popcorn. Oh, how it hurt!

" 'Esther,' whispered Grandpa, 'we're going to the dentist right now!'

" '*I'm* going,' I whispered back. 'You waited all year to see this!'

"So I left in a hurry. But I was no sooner in the dentist's chair, when who should open the door

and wave at me, but your Grandpa Nathan. 'It was a very short movie,' he said laughing.

"He had followed me, Bubeleh, and was I happy to see him!"

"You could really count on him, no matter what, couldn't you, Grandma?"

She gives me a big, squishy hug because she's glad that I understand about mensches. "Do you have to be grown up to be a mensch?" I ask.

"No," says Grandma. "Now get the eggs."

"Isn't one egg enough?"

Grandma looks at me as though I am cuckoo. *She* knows that *I* know that we always use three eggs.

"O.K.," I say sighing, "I'll go . . ."

"Then *go*."

"I'm going," I say. But I can't seem to leave her kitchen.

"It's not so terrible that Mrs Fogelman doesn't call you by your right name," she says. Sometimes I think Grandma can read my mind.

"But that's not all," I say.

"What else?"

"Nothing." I change my mind about telling her the rest, because she would only say, "Mrs Fogelman's a good person and a nice person, Bubeleh. She probably has sorrow in her heart."

"Mrs Fogelman's a good person and a nice person, Bubeleh. She probably has sorrow in her heart," Grandma says anyhow.

I ring Mrs Fogelman's bell.

"Well, well," she says, opening the door and looking through her mail instead of at me. "If it isn't Lees."

I wonder how she would like it if I called her Mrs Foofooman? "My name is Lisa, Mrs Fogelman," I say as politely as I can. "My grandma would like to borrow two eggs, please."

"Come in, Lisa," she says, unfolding a letter, "but don't touch anything."

"I'm not going to −" touch anything, I start to say. But she's already getting the eggs.

"Here, Lees," she says, handing them to me, "now be sure to help Grandma!"

"I *always* help my grandma," I say. "And my name isn't *Lees*!"

"Really?" she says, as though she doesn't believe me. "Well, see you later. Now don't give your grandma any trouble!"

I *never* give Grandma trouble. I do not like Mrs Fogelman and I hope she changes her mind about coming to dinner.

After I set the table and Grandma puts up the chicken, we sample the chopped liver on crackers and look at Grandma's photo album.

"What's that?" I say, pointing to something blurry Grandpa Nathan is holding in an old snapshot.

"A dog," says Grandma. "Grandpa called him Zeke."

"I didn't know you had a dog, Grandma."

"He wasn't ours. Grandpa Nathan found him in the street one day. 'Zeke's lost,' he said. 'So I'll love him until I find his owner.'

"Zeke howled day and night, and he wasn't even housebroken. But your grandpa cared for him like for a new baby. And when he finally found the owners and learned they were poor, he bought them a whole case of dog food."

"Zeke could count on him," I say. "And so could Zeke's family."

Grandma Esther smiles, and this time *I* give *her* a big squishy hug. I hope I'll be a mensch one day.

After the pictures, Grandma gets the checkers. I am just about to double jump her when someone knocks on the back door. I hope it is not Mrs Fogelman. Grandma opens the door. "Come in, Ida," I hear her say. Ida is Mrs Fogelman's first name. "Have some tea."

"I can't drink or eat, Esther," she says. "I'm too nervous. Arty's coming to town." Arty is Mrs Fogelman's grown son. "They're leaving the kids with me for three days."

"Oh, how nice!" says Grandma.

"It would be nice for you, Esther. But for me . . . well, I don't get along so well with children . . . Sometimes I don't even know what to say to them . . . even when Arty was little, that's how I was."

Suddenly she begins to cry, and I know it's not the onion kind of crying.

"Lisa," calls Grandma, "please bring Mrs Fogelman some Kleenex."

I don't feel like doing anything for Mrs Fogelman, so I pretend not to hear.

"Lisa!" Grandma calls again. "I said to bring —"

"Oh, all right," I say, and I get it. But Mrs Fogelman is already wiping her face with Grandma's towel. Her hair is in her eyes, and she is sniffling. Maybe Grandma is right. Maybe there *is* sorrow in her heart. But I don't care.

23

"Here, Ida," Grandma says. "Have some chopped liver."

"Delicious," Mrs Fogelman says. I guess her appetite is back.

"Lisa helped me," Grandma says proudly. "She's a big help. Say, Bubeleh, maybe you can come up with some ideas for when Mrs Fogelman's grandchildren are here."

I feel like saying, "I don't want to give ideas to your bossy neighbour!" But instead I say, "I can't think of anything."

"Well," says Mrs Fogelman, helping herself to more liver, "if you think of anything, let me know, Lees."

"My friends call me Lisa," I say grumpily.

Mrs Fogelman takes another cracker. "I guess it's a habit for me to give people nicknames. I always called Arthur Arty."

"You always call Grandma Esther, Esther," I point out.

"Maybe I just give nicknames to children," she says sighing. "Arty never liked it, either." She blows her nose, then puts the tissue in her apron pocket.

Suddenly I remember when I was little and the bigger kids played dressing-up. I kept telling them they looked "super fantastic" until one day Suzie said, "You and your 'super fantastic!' I'm only wearing my mom's old apron. You sound weird!" But I was only trying to be friendly.

Mrs Fogelman takes a tissue and begins to crumple it. "How old are you?" she asks softly.

I tell her.

"What do you do at Grandma's?"

"Grandma tells me stories. We play checkers and cook and have a nice time."

She is quiet for a long while. Then she says, "My grandsons are younger than you. And I'm – I'm not used to telling stories." Her voice sounds very wrinkly. "And Mr Fogelman's a better cook than I am. And I haven't played checkers in fifty years . . ." She looks right at me. "What do *you* think?"

"Well," I say, "you could practise some stories on me at dinner. I'll – I'll sit next to you."

Mrs Fogelman smiles a little smile.

"And afterwards I'll remind you how to play checkers."

Her smile gets a little bigger.

"And after that I'll tell you about the egg part of making chopped liver – how to hard boil and mash. And I'll even show you my new folk dance."

Her smile gets still bigger.

At dinner she tells me a funny story. "Your grandsons will like it," I say.

She puts her hand on mine. It is cosy and warm. "Esther," I hear her say to Grandma, "your granddaughter Lisa is a real mensch!"

I wouldn't even have minded if she'd called me Lees.

WHEN HITLER STOLE PINK RABBIT

Judith Kerr

It is 1933 and Anna's family have had to leave their home in Berlin to escape the Nazis, led by Adolf Hitler, who are beginning to take over Germany. Papa escaped first, but now Anna, Max and Mama have joined him in the safety of Zurich, Switzerland.

Papa had reserved rooms for them in the best hotel in Zurich. It had a revolving door and thick carpets and lots of gold everywhere. As it was still only ten o'clock in the morning they ate another breakfast while they talked about everything that had happened since Papa had left Berlin.

At first there seemed endless things to tell him, but after a while they found it was nice just being together without saying anything at all. While Anna and Max ate their way through two different kinds of croissants and four different kinds of jam, Mama

27

and Papa sat smiling at each other. Every so often they would remember something and Papa would say, "Did you manage to bring the books?" or Mama would say, "The paper rang and they'd like an article from you this week if possible." But then they would relapse back into their contented, smiling silence.

At last Max drank the last of his hot chocolate, wiped the last crumbs of croissant off his lips and said, "What shall we do now?"

Somehow nobody had thought.

After a moment Papa said, "Let's go and look at Zurich."

They decided first of all to go to the top of a hill overlooking the city. The hill was so steep that you had to go by funicular – a kind of lift on wheels that went straight up at an alarming angle. Anna had never been in one before and spent her time between excitement at the experience and anxious scrutiny of the cable for signs of fraying. From the top of the hill you could see Zurich

clustered below at one end of an enormous blue lake. It was so big that the town seemed quite small by comparison, and its far end was hidden by mountains. Steamers, which looked like toys from this height, were making their way round the edge of the lake, stopping at each of the villages scattered along the shores and then moving on to the next. The sun was shining and made it all look very inviting.

"Can anyone go on those steamers?" asked Max. It was just what Anna had been going to ask.

"Would you like to go?" said Papa. "So you shall – this afternoon."

Lunch was splendid, at a restaurant with a glassed-in terrace overlooking the lake below, but Anna could not eat much. Her head was feeling

swimmy, probably from getting up so early, she thought, and though her nose had stopped running her throat was sore.

"Are you all right?" asked Mama anxiously.

"Oh yes!" said Anna, thinking of the steamer trip in the afternoon. Anyway, she was sure it was just tiredness.

There was a shop selling picture postcards next door to the restaurant and she bought one and sent it to Heimpi while Max sent one to Gunther.

"I wonder how they're getting on with the elections," said Mama. "Do you think the Germans will really vote for Hitler?"

"I'm afraid so," said Papa.

"They might not," said Max. "A lot of the boys at my school were against him. We might find tomorrow that almost no one had voted for Hitler and then we could all go home again, just as Onkel Julius said."

"It's possible," said Papa, but Anna could see that he didn't really think so.

The steamer trip in the afternoon was a great success. Anna and Max stayed on the open deck in spite of the cold wind and watched the other traffic on the lake. Apart from the steamers there were private motor launches and even a few rowing boats. Their steamer went chug-chugging along from village to village on one side of the lake. These all looked very pretty, with their neat

houses nestling among the woods and the hills. Whenever the steamer was getting near a landing stage it hooted loudly to let everyone in the village know that it was coming, and quite a lot of people got on and off each time. After about an hour it suddenly steamed straight across the lake to a village on the other side and then made its way back to Zurich where it had started.

As she walked back to the hotel through the noise of cars and buses and clanging trams Anna found she was very tired, and her head felt swimmy again. She was glad to get back to the hotel room which she shared with Max. She still was not hungry and Mama thought she looked so weary that she tucked her into bed straightaway. As soon as Anna put her head down on the pillow her whole bed seemed to take off and float away in the darkness with a chug-chugging noise which might have been a boat, or a train, or a sound coming from her own head.

Anna's first impression when she opened her eyes in the morning was that the room was far too bright. She closed them again quickly and lay quite still, trying to collect herself. There was a murmur of voices at the other end of the room and also a rustling sound which she could not identify. It must be quite late and everyone else must be up.

She opened her eyes again cautiously and this time the brightness heaved and swayed and finally rearranged itself into the room she knew, with Max, still in his pyjamas, sitting up in the other bed and Mama and Papa standing close by. Papa had a newspaper and this was what was making the rustling sound. They were talking quietly because they thought she was still asleep. Then the room gave another heave and she closed her eyes again and seemed to drift away somewhere while the voices went on.

Someone was saying ". . . so they've got a majority . . ." Then the voice faded away and another − (or was it the same one?) − said ". . . enough votes to do what he wants . . ." and then unmistakably Max, very unhappily, ". . . so we shan't be going back to Germany . . . so we shan't be going back to Germany . . ." Had he really said it three times? Anna opened her eyes with a great effort and said "Mama!" At once one of the figures detached itself from the group and came towards her and suddenly Mama's face appeared quite close to hers. Anna said "Mama!" again and then all at once she was crying because her thoat was so sore.

After this everything became vague. Mama and Papa were standing by her bed looking at a thermometer. Papa had his coat on. He must have gone out to buy the thermometer specially. Someone said, "A hundred and four", but it couldn't be her temperature they were talking about because she couldn't remember having it taken.

Next time she opened her eyes there was a man with a little beard looking at her. He said, "Well, young lady," and smiled and as he smiled his feet left the ground and he flew to the top of the wardrobe where he changed into a bird and sat croaking, "Influenza" until Mama shooed him out of the window.

Then suddenly it was night and she asked Max to get her some water, but Max was not there, it was Mama in the other bed. Anna said, "Why are you sleeping in Max's bed?" Mama said, "Because you're ill," and Anna felt very glad because if she was ill it meant that Heimpi would be coming to look after her. She said, "Tell Heimpi . . ." but then she was too tired to remember the rest, and the next time she looked the man with the little beard was there again and she didn't like him because he was upsetting Mama by saying, "Complications" over and over again. He had done something to the back of Anna's neck and had made it all swollen and sore, and now he was feeling it with his hand. She said, "Don't do that!" quite sharply, but he took no notice and tried to make her drink something horrible. Anna was going to push it away, but then

she saw that it was not the man with the beard after all but Mama, and her blue eyes looked so fierce and determined that it didn't seem worth resisting.

After this the world grew a little steadier. She began to understand that she had been ill for some time, that she still had a high temperature and that the reason she felt so awful was that all the glands in her neck were enormously swollen and tender.

"We must get the temperature down," said the doctor with the beard.

Then Mama said, "I'm going to put something on your neck to make it better."

Anna saw some steam rising from a basin.

"It's too hot!" she cried. "I don't want it!"

"I won't put it on too hot," said Mama.

"I don't want it!" screamed Anna. "You don't know how to look after me! Where's Heimpi? Heimpi wouldn't put hot steam on my neck!"

"Nonsense!" said Mama, and suddenly she was holding a steaming pad of cotton wool against her own neck. "There," she said, "if it's not too hot for me it won't be too hot for you" – and she clapped it firmly on Anna's neck and quickly wrapped a bandage round it.

It was terribly hot but just bearable.

"That wasn't so bad, was it?" said Mama.

Anna was much too angry to answer and the room was beginning to spin again, but as she drifted off into vagueness she could just hear Mama's voice: "I'm going to get that temperature down if it kills me!"

After this she must have dozed or dreamed because suddenly her neck was quite cool again and Mama was unwrapping it.

"And how are you, fat pig?" said Mama.

"Fat pig?" said Anna weakly.

Mama very gently touched one of Anna's swollen glands.

"This is fat pig," she said. "It's the worst of the lot. The one next to it isn't quite so bad – it's called slim pig. And this one is called pink pig and this is baby pig and this one . . . what shall we call this one?"

"Fräulein Lambeck," said Anna and began to laugh. She was so weak that the laugh sounded more like a cackle but Mama seemed very pleased just the same.

Mama kept putting on the hot fomentations and it was not too bad because she always made jokes about fat pig and slim pig and Fräulein Lambeck, but though her neck felt better Anna's temperature still stayed up. She would wake up feeling fairly normal but by lunchtime she would be giddy and by the evening everything would have become vague and confused. She got the strangest ideas. She was frightened of the wallpaper and could not bear to be alone. Once when Mama left her to go downstairs for supper she thought the room was getting smaller and smaller and cried because she thought she would be squashed. After this Mama had her supper on a tray in Anna's room. The doctor said, "She can't go on like this much longer."

Then one afternoon Anna was lying staring at the curtains. Mama had just drawn them because it was getting dark and Anna was trying to see what shapes the folds had made. The previous evening they had made a shape like an ostrich, and as Anna's temperature went up she had been able to see the ostrich more and more clearly until at last she had been able to make him walk all round the room. This time she thought perhaps there might be an elephant.

Suddenly she became aware of whispering at the other end of the room. She turned her head with difficulty. Papa was there, sitting with Mama, and they were looking at a letter together. She could not hear what Mama was saying, but she could tell from the sound of her voice that she was excited and upset. Then

Papa folded the letter and put his hand on Mama's, and Anna thought he would proably go soon but he didn't – he just stayed sitting there and holding Mama's hand. Anna watched them for a while until her eyes became tired and she closed them. The whispering voices had become more quiet and even. Somehow it was a very soothing sound and after a while Anna fell asleep listening to it.

When she woke up she knew at once that she had slept for a long time. There was something else, too, that was strange, but she could not quite make out what it was. The room was dim except for a light on the table by which Mama usually sat, and Anna thought she must have forgotten to switch it off when she went to bed. But Mama had not gone to bed. She was still sitting there with Papa just as they had done before Anna went to sleep. Papa was still holding Mama's hand in one of his and the folded letter in the other.

"Hello, Mama. Hello, Papa," said Anna. "I feel so peculiar."

Mama and Papa came over to her bed at once and Mama put a hand on her forehead. Then she popped the thermometer in Anna's mouth. When she took it out again she did not seem to be able to believe what she saw. "It's normal!" she said. "For the first time in four weeks it's normal!"

"Nothing else matters," said Papa and crumpled up the letter.

After this Anna got better quite quickly. Fat pig, slim pig, Fräulein Lambeck and the rest gradually shrank and her neck stopped hurting. She began to eat again and to read. Max came and played cards with her when he wasn't out somewhere with Papa, and soon she was allowed to get out of bed for a little while and sit in a chair. Mama had to help her walk the few steps across the room but she felt very happy sitting in the warm sunshine by the window.

Outside the sky was blue and she saw that the people in the street below were not wearing overcoats. There was a lady selling tulips at a stall on the opposite pavement and a chestnut tree at the corner was in full leaf. It was spring. She was amazed how much everything had changed during her illness. The people in the street seemed pleased with the spring weather too and several bought flowers from the stall. The lady selling tulips was round and dark-haired and looked a little bit like Heimpi.

Suddenly Anna remembered something. Heimpi had been going to join them two weeks after they left Germany. Now it must be more than a month. Why hadn't she come? She was going to ask Mama, but Max came in first.

"Max," said Anna, "why hasn't Heimpi come?"

Max looked taken aback. "Do you want to go back to bed?" he said.

"No," said Anna.

"Well," said Max, "I don't know if I'm meant to tell you, but quite a lot happened while you were ill."

"What?" asked Anna.

"You know Hitler won the elections," said Max. "Well, he very quickly took over the whole government, and it's just as Papa said it would be –

nobody's allowed to say a word against him. If they do they're thrown into jail."

"Did Heimpi say anything against Hitler?" asked Anna with a vision of Heimpi in a dungeon.

"No, of course not," said Max. "But Papa did. He still does. And so of course no one in Germany is allowed to print anything he writes. So he can't earn any money and we can't afford to pay Heimpi any wages."

"I see," said Anna, and after a moment she added, "are we poor, then?"

"I think we are, a bit," said Max. "Only Papa is going to try to write for some Swiss papers instead – then we'll be all right again." He got up as though to go and Anna said quickly, "I wouldn't have thought Heimpi would mind about money. If we had a little house I think she'd want to come and look after us anyway, even if we couldn't pay her much."

"Yes, well, that's another thing," said Max. He hesitated before he added, "We can't get a house because we haven't any furniture."

"But . . ." said Anna.

"The Nazis have pinched the lot," said Max. "It's called confiscation of property. Papa had a letter last week." He grinned. "It's been rather like one of those awful plays where people keep rushing in with bad news. And on top of it all there were you, just about to kick the bucket . . ."

"I wasn't going to kick the bucket!" said Anna indignantly.

"Well, I knew you weren't, of course," said Max, "but that Swiss doctor has a very gloomy imagination. Do you want to go back to bed now?"

"I think I do," said Anna. She was feeling rather weak and Max helped her across the room. When she was safely back in bed she said, "Max, this . . . confiscation of property, whatever it's called – did the Nazis take everything – even our things?"

Max nodded.

Anna tried to imagine it. The piano was gone . . . the dining-room curtains with the flowers . . . her bed . . . all her toys which included her stuffed Pink Rabbit. For a moment she felt terribly sad about Pink Rabbit. It had had embroidered black eyes – the original glass ones had fallen out years before – and an endearing habit of collapsing on its paws. Its fur, though no longer very pink, had been soft and familiar. How could she ever have chosen to pack that characterless woolly dog in its stead? It had been a terrible mistake, and now she would never be able to put it right.

"I always knew we should have brought the games compendium," said Max. "Hitler's probably playing Snakes and Ladders with it this very minute."

"And snuggling my Pink Rabbit!" said Anna and laughed. But some tears had come into her eyes and were running down her cheeks all at the same time.

"Oh well, we're lucky to be here at all," said Max.

"What do you mean?" asked Anna.

Max looked carefully past her out of the window.

"Papa heard from Heimpi," he said with elaborate casualness. "The Nazis came for all our passports the morning after the elections."

THE JUDGEMENT

Michael Rosen

Loeb became a Rabbi – but not just an ordinary Rabbi. He became one of the most famous Rabbis in all Europe. His name passed the lips of the most famous and brilliant people of his day. Among his friends were the great astronomers, Tycho Brahe and John Kepler. He became renowned for his clever thoughts and wise actions. He helped people who came before him and solved arguments between them.

In one large shop there were two little shops separated by a very thin wooden wall. One of them was owned by a neat little pork butcher, called Houdek who was, of course, not Jewish, because Jews don't eat pork. The other owned by Polner, an old second-hand clothes dealer who, like plenty of other second-hand clothes dealers before and since *was* Jewish. The wooden wall between the two shops was splintered and cracked and the neat little butcher, Houdek, and the second-hand clothes man, Polner, could hear and even see what the other was up to.

One day Houdek the butcher put his eye next to a hole in the wood and watched Polner the second-hand clothes man counting out his money at the end of the day: the day's takings, as they say. The butcher made a note of exactly how much it came to, and then dashed off to the police.

"Fourteen gold ducats, four silver marks and forty-six groats have been stolen from me. I beg you to search the shopkeepers round and about where I work. I am sure one of them has robbed me of my takings, officer."

.The police hurried down to the market area and ordered every shopkeeper to stay just where he stood. Then, one by one they searched the shopkeepers' wallets and purses. When they came to Polner, there in his wallet were fourteen gold ducats, four silver marks and forty-six groats — exactly the same money that Houdek the butcher had said he had lost.

"Right, we'll have you," said the police to Polner, "you can come with us. You're under arrest."

"But this is my money," said Polner. "This is the money I've taken from selling old clothes all day. This for the woman's hat, the silver for the breeches — it was a good price — they were leather."

"That's easily enough said," called out Houdek. "I know, and you know you haven't had a customer all day, while I've sold ribs, chops, trotters and liver all day long."

By now there was a crowd round, with everyone calling the odds, some saying Polner had stolen the money and some saying Houdek was lying. The two men were taken before a judge who, at the best of times found it difficult to remember which hand was right and which was left. He listened to the two shopkeepers and couldn't really make head nor tail of it.

His clerk whispered in his ear, "Why not send for Rabbi Loeb, this is the sort of thing he might help out on."

So, the Rabbi was sent for and came. The judge was happy to become a spectator.

"You sir," Rabbi Loeb said to Houdek the butcher, "do you have any coins of your own about you?"

"I do," said the butcher.

"Fetch me two pans of hot water," said Loeb to the clerk.

The court rustled with whispers while the clerk fetched the pans as soon as he could.

"Now drop these coins of yours into one of these pans here," said Loeb, and Houdek did just that.

"Now drop the money that we are arguing about into the other pan," he said to the police, and they did that too.

"And now we know the truth," Loeb said.

There was silence. Heads turned towards each other with questioning eyes.

"Now we know the truth," said Loeb. "The second-hand clothes dealer did not steal the money."

"Oh yes," said Houdek angrily, "and how do we know that? Magic? What are you? A witch?"

"No, my friend," the Rabbi said, "look at the surface of the water that has your coins in."

Houdek stepped forward and looked.

"Well? What do you see?"

"Fatty stuff," said Houdek.

"And how about the water in the pan where you put the money we're arguing about?"

Houdek looked again. "Hmph," he said.

"Well?" said Loeb.

"Nothing much," said Houdek.

"Exactly," Loeb said, "then it can't be your money, can it? Your money has meat fat on it."

Houdek stared around him at a court now full of smiles and nods. The judge and the police followed him to the pans of hot water to see the meaty grease on the surface of one and nothing on the other.

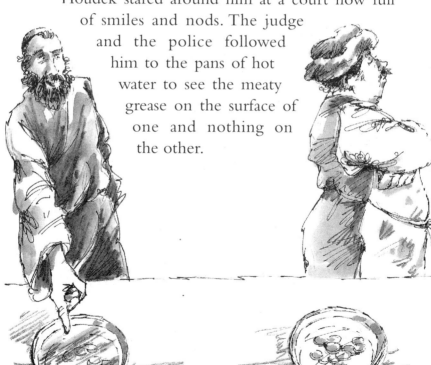

"So, my man," said the judge, "you have falsely accused this dealer in second-hand clothes. You have wasted my time, the police's time and this whole court's time – all for nothing. I won't send you to prison, that'll cost us even more. You can pay the very sum you say you were robbed of into this court and you can pay that very same sum to Polner the second-hand clothes dealer for the pain you have caused him. I don't remember exactly how much that was, but I'm sure you do. The court may rise."

And everyone left the court laughing and mocking Houdek the butcher.

ELIJAH AT THE DOOR

Deborah Freeman

Rachel was having her bath. Ruth watched admiringly. Ruth was only seven, and still had much to learn from Rachel who was nine. Ruth only hoped that one day Sarah, who was four, would grow up and want to learn things from her.

On this particular eve of Pesach, Rachel taught Ruth the following: if you were extremely careful, it was possible to have a bath yet keep your glasses on. With enormous skill, Rachel wet the tips of her fingers, and washed her face – without even getting her spectacles wet!

Rachel, Ruth and Sarah came from an unusual family, gifted in many wonderful ways.

At five o'clock Ruth had her bath. Then she put on her new shot-silk dress. Mummy always bought them new clothes for Pesach. Such a shame no one in the shops knew what Pesach was. They lived in a beautiful city, but in all of its hilly streets, between its museum, its colleges and parks, were scattered no more than one hundred Jewish families.

And out of those, Ruth used to tell people proudly, "We are the only ones who Do Everything."

Well. You may or may not know, but for Jews who *Do Everything*, Pesach is the time of year at which they are the busiest. This year was no exception. There were a million and one things to be Done.

In the magical hours leading up to the Seder Night, when fourteen people would sit round the table, Rachel and Ruth had to play the Pesach game they'd invented. You skipped up and down the hall, backwards and forwards. Then you found that with every skip and hop the evening ahead got more exciting.

"Ruth," Mummy said, stalking warily between her galloping daughters, "even though you're in your best dress, do one more job for me, please. I want you to dry the glass dishes on the draining-board, then bring them in to the dining-room. Put one out for each person. Then go and get wine glasses out of the sideboard. Put a wine glass in each little glass saucer. This year, let's have a Seder without any wine being spilt!"

Ruth was already in a running mood, so she brought the dishes and glasses in one at a time, retracing her steps merrily between each one. It was daylight when she began, but to her horror, Ruth realized that by the time she came to the eleventh saucer and wine glass, she was having to run from the kitchen through the hall in the dark. It had become night outside. And there was nobody left in the hall to protect her.

Sarah had been sent to have a sleep, being only four years old. She'd complained bitterly. But Mummy had said, "You'll never stay awake till the end, if you don't sleep now." Rachel was helping both grannies wind their wool away. Green wool for one granny, rust-coloured for the other.

In the time it had taken to become dark, the hall had changed. Instead of being the heart of a happy house, busy as an ants' nest with preparations, it had become scary. Being Jewish didn't help with everything. Ruth was only seven, but she'd already discovered that.

In a wine-coloured pouffe in the long hall, lived two dangerous dwarfs. Ruth had never seen them. She only thought they were there on the rare occasions all the family ate festively in the dining-room, and she was sent through the hall to the kitchen. Alone. On such occasions, the dwarfs, who slept peacefully at all other times, stirred, rubbed their eyes, snorted, and would have jumped out of the pouffe and done goodness knows what if Ruth didn't scamper as fast as her legs would carry her. Which, I'm glad to say, this time she did. She was the one who helped Mummy put the finishing touches to the Passover table.

"It looks so beautiful," Ruth said to Mummy. "I'm going to remember it like this – for the rest of my life."

The candlesticks gleamed in the middle of the table. Dishes of purple horseradish, crystal cups with slices of cucumber and sprigs of parsley. The white and gold embroidered cover for the Matzo – the unleavened bread which Jews eat at Passover time. The best salad bowl, with its white and floral patterns, gently ridged gold edges.

Beside the candlesticks, in the middle of the table, was a large goblet already brimful with wine.

"What's that for?" asked Ruth.

"It's for Elijah," said Daddy, coming smartly into the room. He looked over the Seder table with pride. There were no other Jews in this city who kept as many of the traditions as Ruth's family kept, so you could be absolutely sure this was the most exciting table for miles around. Daddy came over to Ruth and beamed at her.

"You look very pretty, my dear," he said, and patted her gently on the back of her auburn hair.

"Who's Elijah?" asked Ruth, with a slight sinking feeling. There was no chance, was there, that he might turn out to be one of the dwarfs that lived in the hall?

Mummy and Daddy looked at each other, smiling.

"There's a custom of filling a goblet of wine for Elijah. You know. The Prophet. The *idea* is that he comes in the middle of the Seder, and drinks the wine," explained Daddy.

Mummy and Daddy seemed cheerful as ever, obviously not worried about a thing.

"In fact," Mummy added, "I'm surprised you don't remember. Because last year Rachel opened the door for him to come in, and you cried, so we promised you that this year it would be your turn."

"But will he really come if I open the door?"

asked Ruth. She was a little bit concerned, never having known a prophet before. She wanted to ask if by "prophet," they in fact meant "ghost?" But she was too frightened to ask that!

Daddy said to Ruth, "Look how hard Mummy has worked! Let's all make it the best Seder yet!"

So Ruth stopped thinking about Elijah.

It has to be said that this Seder was a wonderful success. Daddy sang the Haggadah, the story of when the Children of Israel came out of Egypt, after they'd been slaves to Pharaoh. Pesach was all about people being free, and happy, and singing songs which had been sung for hundreds of years. After a glass or two of sweet red wine, the Grannies were terribly cheerful. They reminisced about the long lives they had lived, the countries they had lived in, the Pesach feasts of the past.

One by one the visitors to the Seder joined in the singing, the eating and the merriment. Among them were the Silver family, including all three children, two of whom were twins. Ruth wondered if there was anything about being a twin which made you have a runny nose. She knew it was rude to ask a question like that, so she stored the question away in her head, along with all the other unanswered questions about Pesach. Such as: who is Elijah? And is he really ever likely to turn up here?

The other visitors to the glittering feast were the Leveys. This couple were members of the Jewish community, but they themselves didn't observe

much. For Jews, observing didn't mean what it meant for other people. Other people observed the stars, or views; Jews observed laws and traditions. On a night like tonight, all that observing meant you were part of a gigantic festival, except that unlike the sort of festivals they had in school, which felt quite lukewarm, this one was a blaze of colour. New dresses, and the best dishes. The Grannies added yellows, oranges and purples with their lemon curd, carrot jam and beetroot jam. The Pesach jams glistened in their crystal dishes. The tablecloth was the very best one. It was embroidered all over in purples and pinks, greens and browns, with roses and patterns, trellises and lovely loops.

The Leveys didn't seem to enjoy the singing as much as everyone else. Ruth asked Mrs Levey, "Are you enjoying our Seder?" Mrs Levey nodded politely. She said gravely, "Very much indeed." But you couldn't help noticing that every ten minutes or so, the Leveys took it in turns to look at their watches.

Daddy turned the page of the Haggadah. He reached out towards Elijah's silver goblet, and began to sing the part that meant, among other things: "Hi there, Elijah. Welcome to our Seder." It was time to invite the Prophet to join them. Mummy nodded encouragingly at Ruth. Rachel smiled magnanimously, remembering that last year it had been her turn. Ruth glanced towards Sarah, fearful in case Sarah demanded to be allowed instead. But Sarah, she noted with satisfaction, had fallen asleep with her pretty head on a yellow serviette.

"What do I do?"

"Go to the front door and open it."

Ruth stood up, marched away from the candle-light and warmth, out into the cold hall.

Glancing fearfully in the direction of the sleeping dwarfs, Ruth placed her hand on the doorknob. As she did so she heard the tread of heavy footsteps on the other side of the door. She stood frozen with fear.

"Well?" they all called from the safety of the feast. And that was when the doorbell rang. Loudly.

Ruth's screams of fright brought Mummy and Daddy running into the hall.

"Elijah! He's here! He rang the bell."

Mrs Levey, checking her wristwatch yet again, moved to the front door and opened it.

"I think it's our taxi," she said, apologetically.

Of course, once she realized the man at the door drove a taxi, and wasn't a prophet, Ruth stopped being afraid. The Leveys left, and the evening continued. Then they cracked nuts, peeled oranges and drank tea which they stirred with special Pesach teaspoons. If you want to know what it was like, try and imagine this: imagine swinging in a magic hammock which is made of a beautiful floral tablecloth; Hebrew words; books with wine spilt on them from past Seders; jams; silver goblets of wine; parents, sisters and grandmothers, and endless, endless melodies!

When they came to tuck her up in bed, her parents told Ruth what a clever girl she'd been, opening the door for Elijah. Ruth wanted to ask so many questions. Who was Elijah? Were Prophets real? Would he *ever* come to a Seder Night? Anywhere in the world? Were there two malign dwarfs in the pouffe in the hall?

Mummy said, "Goodnight, darling. Sleep well."

And Daddy said, "Pesach is a time for telling stories. One day, when you're grown up, maybe you'll tell this story. How you opened the door for Elijah the Prophet, just as the doorbell rang. Goodnight, darling. God Bless."

SPECIAL FRIDAYS

Tamar Hodes

I grew up in South Africa in the shadow of Table Mountain. Each morning I opened my bedroom window to the sight of this constant rock – constant, but always changing. Sometimes grey, sometimes purple; sometimes stark against the sky, sometimes with wisps of cloud hanging over it, like an old man's hair.

"The tablecloth is on the mountain today," Amina would say. Amina was our maid. She was young and very beautiful, her coffee-coloured skin silky and smooth. Her hair was black and always tied up at the back (mother insisted on it) and she wore pale pastel shades of apron, one day lemon, another pink. She reminded me of sugar-almonds – fresh, clean, appealing. Amina was my closest friend.

Mother and Father ran a grocery store in the centre of Cape Town. I liked going there when I was allowed to: there were tins of meat neatly lined up and sweets in huge glass jars. But I wasn't taken there very often, in case I interfered with business. My life was with Amina, at home, playing, swimming in the pool, listening to her tales, learning her songs. I loved my days with Amina. I had not yet started school because in South Africa you wait until you are six. Six blissful years with Amina.

And of course, we had our special secret.

Every Friday morning, for as long as I could remember, Amina had dressed me up. "Come now, Master Joel, we are going to our special Friday morning service."

I knew the routine. This meant smart trousers and shirt, and worst of all, having my face scrubbed. This was no joke. My skin held taut with one hand, she would use the other to launch a soap and flannel attack which seemed to last forever and left my cheeks stinging. She would change into a nice dress and off we would go, hand in hand, along the dusty road, listening to the cicadas clicking in the bushes, stopping to pick a bougainvillaea flower and feel its dryness in my hand.

It was a long walk to the mosque, where Muslims prayed, but it was worth it. Inside, we were always warmly welcomed. I sat with Amina behind a screen. There were other maids there with the children they looked after, Jewish children, like me. I knew them all – Sammy, Rebecca, little

Jackie Shapiro with his runny nose. We loved the singing, loved to watch the men kneel on woven mats and pray, bow and chant. It seemed to me not very different from the synagogue where we sometimes went on Saturday mornings – we couldn't always go because of the shop – the women and children behind a screen, the praying, the singing, the sense of joy.

Then the long walk home, clutching the bag of sweets which Amina's friend always gave me. Amina would remind me, "Remember, Master Joel, don't tell your mummy about our special

Fridays. They are our secret. If she found out, we might not be allowed to go any more."

The dreaded day of school approached more quickly than I had thought possible. As Amina put on my new uniform, I wept. I did not want to leave her, would miss her sugar-almond aprons, her lovely smell, her soft skin, her songs and our secret.

The private Jewish school was not too bad. I liked our teacher, Mrs Elias, because she was kind. Well, except when she was cross. Then her neck would flare purple and she would shake with anger.

At the end of our first month there, we had an open day. There were displays of our work and singing for our parents. The headmistress made a speech. Then she decided to demonstrate the brilliance of her pupils. She asked, "What is special about Fridays? Why do we enjoy them so?"

I was surprised. How did she know my secret? Was everyone in on it? I didn't suppose it mattered if I said. Besides, Amina wasn't there and we didn't go together any more, now that I was at school. Mother was there, in her best brown hat. She nodded at me as if egging me on. *Go on, Joel. You can answer the question nicely.* I supposed it was all right. My hand shot up.

"Yes, Joel. What do you do on Fridays?"

"I go to the mosque," I said.

My mother didn't speak on the way home and then I was sent to my room without dinner. I can still remember her voice hissing at Amina in the next room. I heard the maid's sobs and then a few minutes later, the front door closed. I stood on my chair and pulled back the blind. There, below the huge block of Table Mountain, was Amina, her pale lemon apron getting smaller as she disappeared from view.

I have often thought since, about how and why religions are different, and to what extent we can appreciate someone else's without losing our own. I am an adult now and proud to be Jewish, but I have never forgotten Amina.

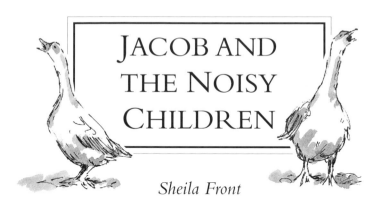

JACOB AND THE NOISY CHILDREN

Sheila Front

Jacob the tailor worked hard for his living. He made clothes for the people of his village. With the money he was able to buy food and comforts for his wife Rivka and their three children.

But each day the children became noisier and noisier. Benjamin teased his sister, Sarah, and they both woke baby Ruth and made her cry. Their small house only had one room and Jacob tried to work while his wife busied herself with the dozens of jobs she always had to do. Round and round the table rushed the children, until Jacob became dizzy. Needles, pins and cottons flew through the air.

One day Jacob could stand it no longer.

"Rivka!" He shouted. "Can't you keep your children quiet?"

"Why are they always *my* children when they are noisy, and *yours* when they are well-behaved?"

complained his wife. "Peace! Jacob. They are only being children."

But matters grew worse and worse. At last in a fit of temper Jacob put on his warm hat and coat and stormed out of the house into the thick snow.

"Where are you going, Jacob?" called Rivka.

"Enough is enough!" her husband shouted over his shoulder. "I'm going to see the Rabbi, he is a wise man. He always knows what to do."

After the morning prayers in the synagogue, Jacob caught up with the Rabbi and walked along with him.

"Well Jacob?" asked the learned man. "How are things with you? That coat you made me is just right for this cold weather."

"I'm glad," said Jacob, "but there's something else on my mind. I'd like to talk to you about it."

"That's why I'm here," said the Rabbi. "Come home with me and we'll talk about your problem over a nice glass of lemon tea."

In his cosy study the samovar steamed and bubbled on the table as the two men talked. Jacob explained all about his noisy children to the Rabbi who listened carefully, nodding his head from time to time.

"I just want a little peace and quiet," said Jacob. "I love my children but they're driving me crazy."

The Rabbi closed his eyes and stroked his beard thoughtfully for a few minutes before giving his reply.

"Jacob, you must go to the market and buy some animals for your children to play with."

"Ah!" said Jacob excitedly, "I see. The pets will keep the children occupied and they will leave me in peace."

"We shall see, Jacob. We shall see," was all the wise man said.

The market was busy and bustling when Jacob arrived. He chose a friendly brown donkey, a lively white goat and a handsome goose, fine pets for his children, he thought. He tethered the goat to the donkey which he rode home, carrying the goose under one arm to stop it flying away.

The journey was a difficult one but well worth it as he saw the delighted surprise of his family when they saw their new pets.

Sure enough, as he had hoped everyone seemed happy. Sarah fed the goat, Benjamin rode the donkey, a little wildly it is true, and baby Ruth gurgled at the goose who made funny noises back at her as if it was talking.

"At last!" said Jacob, raising his eyes thankfully to heaven. "Perhaps now I will have a little peace."

But as time passed the children became more mischievous again. They strayed from home with their pets until Rivka and Jacob warned them of the many dangers and told them to play near the house.

Before long the winter snows began to thaw in the warm spring sunshine. But now not only were the children becoming noisy but the animals too behaved badly. The goat liked to eat everything in sight, the donkey brayed and kicked a lot and the goose cackled, squawked and flapped and one day flew on to the roof, where it had to be rescued by poor Jacob who nearly fell off the ladder.

Once more Jacob was coming to the end of his patience.

The last straw came when the goat butted his bottom as he was chopping logs.

"Enough is enough!" Jacob yelled in pain. The children knew it meant trouble when their father said that. "It's time I went to see the Rabbi again." And rubbing his bruised bottom he set off for the wise man's house.

"Shalom, Jacob," said the Rabbi as he opened the door. "You look tired. Come in for some tea and a chat."

The Rabbi smiled knowingly as he listened to Jacob's story. "This is what you must do," he said at last. "Take the animals back to the market and sell them."

"But Rabbi!" protested Jacob. "You told me to buy them in the first place."

"Never mind, Jacob," replied the wise man. "Just do as I say and we shall see!"

Early next morning, Jacob and Rivka borrowed their neighbour's horse and cart and the whole family set off for the market, taking the greedy goat, the stubborn donkey and the crazy goose with them.

They found kind owners for all the animals, and the children, who were very good-hearted really, let their pets go without too much fuss.

On the way home, Jacob thought about the next day when he would be able to carry on with his work in peace and quiet.

"You see, Rivka," said Jacob happily, as he ironed a new coat. "The Rabbi was right. We must count our blessings. We have a lovely family and see how quiet the children are without those noisy animals."

But Rivka and Sarah and Benjamin were not so sure. After all, the animals may have gone but baby Ruth was on the move.

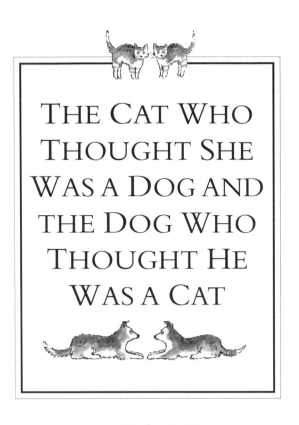

THE CAT WHO THOUGHT SHE WAS A DOG AND THE DOG WHO THOUGHT HE WAS A CAT

Isaac Bashevis Singer

Once there was a poor peasant, Jan Skiba by name. He lived with his wife and three daughters in a one-room hut with a straw roof, far from the village. The house had a bed, a bench bed, and a stove, but no mirror. A mirror was a luxury for a poor peasant. And why would a peasant need a mirror? Peasants aren't curious about their appearance.

But this peasant did have a dog and a cat in his hut. The dog was named Burek and the cat Kot. They had both been born within the same week. As little food as the peasant had for himself and his family, he still wouldn't let his dog and cat go hungry. Since the dog had never seen another dog and the cat had never seen another cat and they saw only each other, the dog thought he was a cat and the cat thought she was a dog. True, they were far from being alike by nature. The dog barked, and the cat meowed. The dog chased rabbits, and the cat lurked after mice. But must all creatures be exactly like their own kind? The peasant's children weren't exactly alike either. Burek and Kot lived on good terms, often ate from the same dish, and tried to mimic each other. When Burek barked, Kot tried to bark along, and when Kot meowed, Burek tried to meow too. Kot occasionally chased rabbits and Burek made an effort to catch a mouse.

The pedlars who bought groats, chickens, eggs, honey, calves, and whatever was available from the peasants in the village never came to Jan Skiba's poor hut. They knew that Jan was so poor he had nothing to sell. But one day a pedlar happened to stray there. When he came inside and began to lay out his wares, Jan Skiba's wife and daughters were bedazzled by all the pretty doodads. From his sack the pedlar drew yellow beads, false pearls, tin earrings, rings, brooches, coloured kerchiefs,

garters, and other such trinkets. But what enthralled the women of the house most was a mirror set in a wooden frame. They asked the pedlar its price and he said a half gulden, which was a lot of money for poor peasants. After a while, Jan Skiba's wife, Marianna, made a proposition to the pedlar. She would pay him five groshen a month for the mirror. The pedlar hesitated a moment. The mirror took up too much space in his sack and there was always the danger it might break. He therefore decided to go along, took the first payment of five groshen from Marianna, and left the mirror with the family. He visited the region often and he knew the Skibas to be honest people. He would gradually get his money back and a profit besides.

The mirror created a commotion in the hut. Until then Marianna and the children had seldom seen themselves. Before they had the mirror they had only seen their reflections in the barrel of water that stood by the door. Now they could see themselves clearly and they began to find defects in their faces, defects they had never noticed before. Marianna was pretty but she had a tooth missing in front and she felt that this made her ugly. One daughter discovered that her nose was too snub and too broad; a second that her chin was too narrow and too long; a third that her face was sprinkled with freckles. Jan Skiba too caught a glimpse of himself in the mirror and grew displeased by his thick lips and his teeth, which protruded like a buck's. That day, the women of the house became so absorbed in the mirror they didn't cook supper, didn't make up the bed, and neglected all the other house-hold tasks. Marianna had heard of a dentist in the big city who could replace a missing tooth, but such things were expensive. The girls tried to console each other that they were pretty enough and that they would find suitors, but they no longer felt as jolly as before. They had been afflicted with the vanity of city girls. The one with the broad nose kept trying to pinch it

together with her fingers to make it narrower; the one with the too-long chin pushed it up with her fist to make it shorter; the one with the freckles wondered if there was a salve in the city that could remove freckles. But where would the money come from for the fare to the city? And what about the money to buy this salve? For the first time the Skiba family deeply felt its poverty and envied the rich.

But the human members of the household were not the only ones affected. The dog and the cat also grew disturbed by the mirror. The hut was low, and the mirror had been hung just above a bench. The first time the cat sprang up on the bench and saw her image in the mirror, she became terribly perplexed. She had never before seen such a creature. Kot's whiskers bristled, she began to meow at her reflection and raised a paw to it, but the other creature meowed back and raised her paw too. Soon the dog jumped up on the bench, and when he saw the other dog, he became wild with rage and shock. He barked at the other dog and showed him his teeth, but the other barked back and bared his fangs too. So great was the distress of Burek and Kot that for the first time in their lives they turned on each other. Burek took a bite out of Kot's throat and Kot hissed and spat at him and clawed his muzzle. They both started to bleed and the sight of blood aroused them so that they nearly killed or crippled each other. The members of the household barely managed to separate them. Because a dog is stronger than a cat, Burek had to be tied outside, and he howled all day and all night. In their anguish, both the dog and the cat stopped eating.

When Jan Skiba saw the disruption the mirror had created in his household, he decided a mirror wasn't what his family needed. "Why look at yourself," he said, "when you can see and admire the sky, the sun, the moon, the stars, and the earth, with all its forests, meadows, rivers and plants?" He took the mirror down from the wall and put it away in the woodshed. When the pedlar came for his monthly installment, Jan Skiba gave him back the mirror and in its stead, bought kerchiefs and slippers for the women. After the mirror disappeared, Burek and Kot returned to normal. Again Burek thought he was a cat and Kot was sure she was a dog. Despite all the defects the girls had found in themselves, they made good marriages. The village rabbi heard what had happened at Jan Skiba's house and he said, "A glass mirror shows only the skin of the body. The real image of a person is in his willingness to help himself and his family and, as far as possible, all those he comes in contact with. This kind of mirror reveals the very soul of the person."

BATATA

Lynne Reid Banks

Fat people can't help being fat.

That's what I believe. Not everyone agrees with me, but I've proved it.

I'm fat. Okay. I was meant to be fat. I've seen pictures of myself all the way since I was born and I have been fat all my life. All except one spell. I call it my thin spell.

It happened when I was ten.

On my tenth birthday I had a party, but it wasn't on our lawn as usual. We had just moved to our new *shikkun vatikim*. That means the houses of the veterans. Not war veterans – kibbutz veterans (though my dad's a war veteran too – he was in Lebanon in the Peace for Galilee war. Just don't get him started on it, that's all. It makes him so mad).

My parents were born in our kibbutz so they have a high veterans' rating. Not as high as my grandparents', but high-ish. So we moved into one of the new houses before a lot of people in my class.

The new house was great. It was one half of a two-family villa. A lovely big living-room, my parents' bedroom, and two little bedrooms for me and my brother. It's good he's a male. If we'd been two girls we'd have had to share and probably ended up strangling each other. Also a kitchenette and bathroom. A real bath. Showers are better for keeping clean but Mum and I like to soak in a hot bath in the winter. Some people think Israel's boiling hot all the time, but it gets really cold up here in the north in wintertime. Luckily my birthday's in summer, so I always have my party outside on our lawn.

Our new house had a great big area in front for the garden. I thought it would be terrific for the party. But the new lawn wasn't ready in time for it.

My mother is the kibbutz gardener, I mean she's the head of that branch, so you'd think she could've got our lawn planted before everyone else's. But when I asked her to, in good time, so it could be nice for my party, she wouldn't. She said it wasn't *kibbutzic* to do something like that, give your family advantages because of your job.

So she planted practically everyone else's lawns before ours, and a week before my birthday our lawn was just a nasty bit of old earth with some stringy lines of grass across it looking like over-grown green barbed-wire, and a big sign saying *Lo lalekhet al hadesheh* – Don't walk on the lawn.

What lawn?

I was really *brogges* about it. So I gave everyone the silent treatment. It was aimed at Mum but it covered everyone in the family. I kept it up for four whole days. Naturally I got lonely and fed up, so to make myself feel a bit better, I ate. Extra.

My brother brought me out of it by making me so mad at him I had to stop not talking. He started calling me *Batata*. That means – well, it's a funny word for potato. It's not even Hebrew, I don't know what language it is, but it certainly means just one thing when someone calls you it: *Fatty*.

I tried to ignore it but I couldn't, because every time I put something in my mouth, he said "Ba–ta–ta!" If no one was about, he'd say it aloud in a maddening singy sort of voice. If anyone, like Mum for instance, was within earshot, he'd just say it with his lips.

In the end I just burst. Not my stomach. My mouth.

We're not allowed to call names in our house. So what about him calling me Batata? Mum said she didn't hear that. Well, she wouldn't − he saw to that! But when I called him Pigface and Donkey's-Backside she sent me to my room and told me if I didn't stop sulking and losing my temper there wouldn't be a party at all.

I sat in my room and cried with rage. I hated my brother, but what else is new? No party − that was new! Well, who cared? What kind of party could it be, anyway, with no lawn to have it on? Indoors? Don't be funny! Imagine eighteen kids crammed indoors in the heat. Our living-room isn't that big. But I wanted a party, a proper party! I cried more. I howled. Then suddenly I stopped.

Being all alone in kibbutz is kind of unusual. Maybe being alone made me go inside myself. Anyhow I got my idea. My fantastic idea!

I would starve myself and get thin.

Was that a great idea, or what? And I made up my mind to do it just at the time when I could really show everyone I meant business. Just before my birthday.

But I had to get into training. I started that evening.

It was the eve of Sabbath. We always go to the *hader okhel* – that's the big dining-hall in the middle of the kibbutz – for supper on *erev Shabbat*. We walk down together as a family and sit together and it's nice – usually.

Mum had let me out of my room after about an hour. I didn't say anything. I just washed my face and put on a clean blouse and combed my hair. I looked at myself in the bathroom mirror. And I suddenly saw that I was a batata. My blouse bulged out at the front and my jeans bulged out at the back and I had a double chin. A potato. That was me.

I stared hard at my fat self and made a promise: this was the very last time that I would see myself looking exactly like this. By tomorrow night I might still be a potato but I'd be a smaller one, because I wasn't going to eat one single thing until then.

In the *hader okhel* there were white tablecloths, a candle on each table, and some flowers. It always looks really nice on Shabbat. We sat there and the others chatted and nibbled soup-almonds and soon the soup came round. I hadn't nibbled even one of the crispy little squares. No one had noticed. But

when they put a big plateful of soup in front of me and I didn't immediately drop a big handful of *shkaydim* in and start *shlupping*, they noticed that all right!

"*Ma yesh?*" asked Dad.

"Nothing. I'm not hungry."

My parents gaped at me. My brother dropped his spoon and his jaw, both.

"Tal's not hungry," he said. "End of the world. Cheerio, goodbye, shalom!"

My mother immediately started to fuss, but Dad gave her a look. "Leave her. If she's not hungry, she's not hungry. Good if she slims down." I felt Mum stiffen. Here it came! "No one should be fat in Israel." Where had we heard *that* before?

"Anyhow she can live off her own fat for a month," said my sweet dear brother. "Like a camel." And he took another handful of soup-almonds.

I kept my cool. Didn't even stick my tongue out. I just sat looking at the soup and thinking, *I am strong and resolute. I am not going to touch a drop.*

The braised beef came on a big dish. It smells stronger and more mouthwatering than chicken, and fills you up more too. And there were pan-fried potatoes, mixed up with little bits of fried onion – my favourite. But I didn't touch so much as one bite. My brother had mine.

Now my mother got worried. "Are you feeling okay?"

"I'm fine, *Ima*," I said lightly. "Just fine."

Afterwards we went home and Mum served her special glazed apple tart. The others ate. Two pieces each. They said how tasty it was. Several times . . . I sat and watched television.

I wasn't feeling real hunger yet. I just thought of my stomach expecting food and not getting any and beginning to shrink. I thought of my fat turning to water and trickling away in the night. I went to bed early without being told so it could begin. But I weighed myself secretly first on my mother's scales.

I won't say how many kilos. A lot though. But I betted it would have been more if I'd weighed myself before supper.

The next day passed more slowly than any day in my life.

I didn't eat. I drank, of course. Even Gandhi drank on his hunger-strikes. I drank tap water, and soda water for a treat.

After twenty-four hours I crept to the bathroom and weighed myself. The needle jumped round and I willed it to stop – *and it did!* I suddenly saw I'd lost 350 grams! I felt light, as if I might float away.

So I kept on not eating.

I expected my family to fuss, at least to notice. But after that first meal, nobody said a thing. This made me *brogges* again (didn't they *care?*) until I caught a look between Mum and Dad and realized they'd *decided* not to say anything. That made me more determined than ever.

Meal followed meal. I smelt the food. I saw it. I longed for it. But I didn't eat it.

Didn't I get hungry?

I'm glad you asked. Answer: in one word, yes. I was half-dead from it. But I knew it was working. I was getting thinner. I felt bad inside from hunger. But I felt good inside too. I even welcomed the suffering.

I kept it up for – wait for it – two whole days. Two and a half, if you count that first night. And then it was my birthday.

As always, Mum left *saciot* beside my bed. Little bags full of sweets and nuts and stuff. One *sacit* for each person in my class. Usually I've finished mine before I even get to school, but today I just put my *sacit* in the wastepaper basket. Strong, or what? Besides, I wanted Mum to find it.

She did.

I saw her later. She was sitting on the little garden tractor, mowing the big lawn in the centre of the kibbutz. I purposely didn't wave, but she veered round and stopped next to me.

"Why did you throw your *sacit* away?"

"I didn't want it."

She narrowed her eyes at me. "What did you have for breakfast?"

"Nothing."

"What's going on with you, Tali?"

"Nothing, why?"

"Are you on a diet?"

"No." (And that was true. On a diet, you eat.)

"If you want to diet – properly – I'll help you."

"I don't need any help, thanks."

"What about the party?"

"Oh! There is going to be a party?"

"What do you think?"

"I've told everyone not to come."

"That's funny," she said, and put her foot down and roared away across the lawn.

After school I did my work-stint in the children's farm. I was so weak from hunger I thought I might faint. Feeding the calves their milk, I could hardly lift the pail.

I'll tell you how hungry I was – you won't believe this. I had to put my hand in the littlest calf's mouth to get him sucking, and then pull his nose down into the milk. As I pulled my hand out of his mouth it passed through the milk, and then, somehow, it was in *my* mouth and *I* was sucking on it just like the calf. I told you you wouldn't believe it. Even I was shocked. I still don't know how it happened.

It scared me, to tell the truth. I don't like anything dirty near my face. There was still some calf's slobber on my hand when it went by itself into my mouth.

I washed hard and swilled my mouth out with about two litres of water and then went home. I was feeling so funny – and you won't believe this, either – I'd sort of forgotten about my birthday and the party and everything. I was all light-headed and the sun made it worse.

I went up the steps and on to the porch. On our main door was a huge notice printed out on a computer:

HAPPY BIRTHDAY TALI!
COME TO THE SWIMMING-POOL.

I gaped.

So that was it! A party by the pool! Cool or what? I forgot my hunger till I got up there. Then I remembered.

Mum and Dad and my brother had brought all the stuff up in the tractor-trailer. The party was under the trees on a trestle with rainbow crêpe paper on it and round it to look festive. The afternoon wind was blowing it about but it looked just wonderful.

The food, though! The food was so special. Mum must have spent hours, not in our kitchenette but secretly in the big kitchen with the big ovens. All sorts of wonderful cakes and cookies, and cold chicken-legs, and some fancy savouries of Grandma's, as well as the regular things like sweets

and nuts and saltsticks and crisps. There was ice cream in a coolbox packed with ice. And lots of different sodas.

My whole family were there, and all my class in their bathing suits, and when they saw me coming they cheered and sang the birthday song:

> *Hayom yom moledet*
> *Hagigah nikhmedet!*
> *Nivarekh otakh*
> *B'yom moladetakh!*

Mum and Dad were just beaming. I nearly

cried, if I'm honest. They'd done it so nicely and
gone to so much trouble and I'd been acting all
brogges and horrible. And now if I stuck to my
guns, I had to hurt them by refusing to eat a single
one of the good things they'd prepared just for me.

Well, what would you have done?

Right. I ate.

I ate some of everything, and drank the soda. We
swam, and played games, and then ate some more.
Then I had to go behind a bush and throw up. My
shrunken stomach just couldn't take it.

While I was sitting behind the bush taking deep
breaths, Mum came looking for me.

She crouched down and said quietly, "This is crazy. You know that. You'll get anorexic and make yourself really ill."

I said, "I don't want to be a batata."

She said, "Eat less. But don't eat nothing."

"If I eat at all, I have to eat lots. I can't help myself."

Mum said, with a lot of feeling, "I do know, Tal. How I know!"

I don't think I mentioned that Mum is fat too.

I said, "Maybe we could diet together."

But she said, "Tali, I've tried. It comes off and goes back on again. I think maybe we're just meant to be fat. We have to like ourselves the way we are."

"Daddy keeps saying nobody in Israel has any right to be fat."

"Yes I know," she said. "It's called Socialism." We laughed. She gave me a big hug. "Are you feeling better?"

"Yes."

"Could you face some ice cream?"

"Yes!"

We came out from behind the bush with our arms round each other. And that was the end of my thin spell.

JUST ENOUGH
IS PLENTY

Barbara Diamond Goldin

Malka's family lived in a village in Poland They were poor, but not so poor. They had candles for the Sabbath, noisemakers for Purim, and spinning-tops for Chanukah.

Mama was busy preparing for tonight, the first of the eight nights of Chanukah. She peeled onions and grated potatoes for the latkes, the potato pancakes.

Malka's younger brother Zalman carved a dreidel, a spinning-top.

"This dreidel will spin the fastest of all," he boasted.

Papa was working long hours in his tailor shop so they could buy more food for the holiday. More potatoes, more onions, more flour, more oil.

For on the first night of Chanukah, Malka's family always invited many guests. But this year only Aunt Hindy and Uncle Shmuel were coming to visit.

"Only two guests?" Malka asked. "Last year, we had so many guests that Papa had to put boards over the pickle barrels to make the table big enough."

"That was last year," Mama said gently. "This year has not been a good one for Papa in the shop. People bring him just a little mending here, a little mending there. He cannot afford to buy new material to sew fancy holiday dresses and fine suits."

"But it's Chanukah," Malka reminded Mama.

Mama patted Malka's shoulder. "Don't worry, Malkaleh. We know how to stretch. We're poor, but not so poor. Now go. Ask Papa if he has a few more coins. I need more eggs for the latkes."

Malka bundled up in her jacket and shawl, her scarf and boots. It was cold and snowy and so windy. The wind chased her all the way to the marketplace.

She raced into Papa's shop. "Mama sent me to buy more eggs."

"More eggs. More this, more that. Soon there will be no kopeks left. Not even one for Chanukah money."

Malka stood still in the doorway. No Chanukah money! Was Papa joking? How could she and Zalman play the dreidel game without even a kopek?

"Malka, don't just stand there. Here. Go buy the eggs," Papa said. "And quickly. Aunt Hindy and Uncle Shmuel will be here soon."

The coins that Papa gave her for the eggs jingled inside her pocket as she ran. Clink. Clink.

Last year, Malka used her Chanukah money to buy candy treats at the marketplace and sleigh rides around the village. Clink. Clink. But this was egg money.

Malka carried the eggs carefully back to the house. She burst into tears when she saw Mama.

"Papa doesn't even have a kopek left for us," she wailed. "No Chanukah money."

"Did Papa say that?"

Malka nodded. Her chin quivered and she couldn't say another word.

Mama wiped her hands on her apron and hugged Malka close. "Was there ever a Chanukah without a kopek for a child to play dreidel with?"

Malka shrugged. She didn't know.

Suddenly, there were loud noises at the door: horses whinnying and stomping and people shouting, "Happy Chanukah!"

"It's them!" Mama cried. "And the latkes aren't fried yet." She ran to the door to welcome Aunt Hindy and Uncle Shmuel, and then she hurried back into the kitchen to fry latkes.

When she finished, she put a coin in the charity box on the shelf, just as she did before each holiday and Sabbath. Malka saw her.

"What if that's our last kopek?" Malka whispered to Zalman.

Then Papa came in from the shop, and the whole family gathered around the little brass menorah on the windowsill.

Papa picked up the shammash, the special candle at the top of the menorah, and chanted the familiar prayers. "Blessed is God who commanded us to light the Chanukah candle . . . Blessed is God who worked miracles for our ancestors long ago . . ."

Zalman tugged at Malka's sleeve. "What miracles?" he asked in a whisper.

"You remember. The oil in the Temple. The oil that burned for eight days instead of only one," Malka explained quickly.

When Papa finished the blessing, he used the shammash to light the first candle-holder in the menorah. The other seven candle-holders were empty, waiting for their turn on the nights to come.

"Sit down, everyone," Mama said, and rushed into the kitchen.

Malka carried platters of latkes to the table as soon as Mama filled them. She saw Papa give Zalman the warning eye as Zalman piled six latkes on his plate.

Papa came into the kitchen. "Is there enough?" he whispered to Mama.

"Just enough," said Mama.

When Malka put the last latke on the table, she and Papa and Mama sat down, too. There was a knock on the door. "Did you invite anyone else?" asked Mama.

"No," said Papa. He got up to see who was there.

It was a pedlar with a large sack on his back. He had white hair and wore a wrinkled black greatcoat and torn boots.

"I saw the Chanukah lights in your window." He spoke softly with his head bowed.

Mama stood up and went to the door. "Come in. Join us. Just like Abraham and Sarah in the Bible, we always have something for the stranger who knocks on our door."

Papa gave Mama a worried look. So did Malka. "We can stretch the 'just enough'," Mama whispered to them. "We're poor, but not so poor."

Mama gave the old man one of her latkes. So did Papa. So did Malka, Aunt Hindy, Uncle Shmuel and even Zalman.

Everyone ate the latkes with apple sauce and sour cream.

"I'm finished, Papa," said Zalman. "Can I play dreidel?"

"Dreidel. I haven't played dreidel in years." The old man leaned forward and beckoned Zalman closer with his finger. "Do you have one?"

"The fastest one in my class," Zalman said.

The old man looked at Papa. "I have a few kopeks. The children could use them to play the dreidel game."

Malka was glad and thanked the pedlar. Now she would have a kopek to play with. But still no candy treats or sleigh rides. No cousins or friends to fill the house.

Malka and Zalman sat on the floor. So did the old man. He took turns with the dreidel, too.

Spin.

Shin. Put one in the pile.

Twirl.

Hay. Take half the coins.

Spin again.

Nun. Take nothing.

Twirl again.

Gimmel. Take all.

Just like the children, the old man made a face when the top landed on *nun*, nothing, and he laughed when the top stopped on *gimmel*, take all.

Then he taught the children songs with words that went around and around again. Once he sang the words loudly and happily, and once he hummed the tune quietly with his eyes closed.

Oy chiri biri biri bim bum bum,
Oy chiri biri biri bim bum bum.

Still singing, he grabbed their hands and they danced in circles, whirling like dreidels themselves.

Giggling and huffing, Malka and Zalman fell to the floor.

The old man reached into his pedlar's sack and drew out one book and then another. He read the stories in his soft voice. Some of them made Malka laugh, others brought tears to her eyes. His stories were about kind people and cruel people, about angels and wonder-working rabbis, about beggars and miracles.

Of all the stories, her favourites were the ones about Elijah the Prophet, who would come back to earth to help someone who was poor but kind-hearted. One time Elijah dressed as a horseman, one time as a beggar, one time as a magician.

"It's as if the whole house were filled with guests," Malka told the pedlar. "With the people of your stories."

Later than night, after Aunt Hindy and Uncle Shmuel left, Papa made a sleeping place for the pedlar. He piled straw by the stove. Before they went to sleep, the old man gave each child a kopek to keep.

"For your Chanukah money," he said. "For some candy treats and sleigh rides around the village."

Malka laughed. "How did you know?"

The pedlar smiled. "I know."

Then Malka and Zalman tumbled into their beds along one of the kitchen walls.

"Good night, Reb . . . Oh, I don't even know your name," Malka said.

"I'll tell you tomorrow," the old man answered.

When Malka awoke in the morning, she lay still in her bed, remembering her dreams about cruel kings and kind farmers, about the people in the pedlar's stories.

"I especially liked the stories about Elijah," Malka said softly, hoping the old man was awake, too. But when she looked for him, she saw an empty pile of straw. He was gone.

"Mama! Papa! Zalman!" Malka called. "Come quickly. The pedlar is gone."

She thought of the winter wind pushing him down the street.

"Oh, I wished he had stayed. Didn't he know Mama can always make plenty out of just enough?" she said to Zalman, who looked disappointed too. "And we don't even know his name."

"But wait," Mama said. "What's that over there? Did he forget something?"

Malka saw the pedlar's sack by the door and ran over to it.

"There's a note," she said. "Mama, what does it say?"

"Just 'Happy Chanukah. This will help you,'" Mama read.

"No name?"

"No. No name."

Malka peeped into the sack. She recognized the book on top. It was the old book with the stories about Elijah.

Malka gasped. Clutching the book, she turned to Mama and Papa and Zalman, "I know who the pedlar is. He's Elijah!"

"Elijah? You really believe that old man is Elijah the Prophet? Oy," Papa said, hitting his head with his hand.

"He could be, Papa," Malka said. "Remember how Elijah left things for the people he visited in those stories?"

"But we are real people, not story-people, Malkaleh. And why would he leave us his whole sackful of books? I'm a tailor, not a book pedlar."

Papa turned to the sack. He took out one book after the other, big books and little books, old books and new books. About halfway down the sack, Papa stopped. He stood up, confused.

"There's a problem?" Mama asked anxiously.

"No, not a problem," Papa said hesitantly. "Just . . ."

Once again he stooped down over the sack. They all crowded around him as he lifted one, two, three bolts of silk and more out of the sack. Purple silk, green silk, dotted silk, silk with stripes and checks and flowers.

"Look what your Elijah gave us this Chanukah!" Papa said to Malka and twirled her happily in the air. "What fancy holiday dresses and fine suits I can make now."

He took Malka's hand and Malka took Zalman's hand and Zalman reached over for Mama. Malka turned to Mama and said, "I'm glad you're so good at making just enough be plenty!"

Laughing, they all began to dance, and sing,

Oy chiri biri biri bim bum bum,
Oy chiri biri biri bim bum bum,
Oy chiri biri biri bim.

THE OPEN DOOR

Miriam Hodgson

Isaac Jacob woke up with a start. The words that came into his head were "Why is this night different from all other nights?"

Was he dreaming? Was he a little boy in Germany again, the youngest at the Passover Seder waiting to ask that question? No, it wasn't a dream, he was in England with a boy of his own. It was time to start the preparations. Tonight was the first night of Passover and there was much to do.

He washed and dressed and got breakfast ready for Hannah, his wife, and the children, Gabriel and Rachel, hindered as always by Juno, the grey Persian cat of incredible beauty. She had eyes the colour of Mycenean gold. Isaac, who was a teacher, never stopped trying to teach her obedience.

"Greedy Beast! Don't go into the pantry. Out, out, go into the garden," he shouted as he opened the door. Juno swished her tail and ran along the track she had made herself across the lawn. She knew her master had a temper.

Before Hannah came downstairs with the children, and family life really began on this day of days, Isaac sat down for a moment with his prayer book and said the morning prayer. Somehow, as always, it restored him and today was a day when everyone needed strength. His face in repose was full of patience and humour. A friend once said that if he ever came face to face with God and found that He looked like Isaac, he would be much cheered by the clear-sighted, twinkling grey-blue eyes, which were so alive and showed such care for everyone.

After breakfast there was an important task to perform. The small pieces of bread, collected the night before as the last of the leavened food in the house, were burned. Now everything was ready to celebrate Passover.

Soon the house was bustling. Gabriel rushed upstairs to fetch from the spare room cupboard the special plates and cutlery that were used only at Passover. Then Rachel washed and dried them. Hannah was cooking the lamb dish. It would be eaten at the special Seder supper that night, to remind everyone of the sacrifice of the Passover. When the children of Israel were slaves in Egypt the Lord smote the Egyptians with plague and passed over the houses of the Israelites. He brought them safely out of slavery to freedom, through the Red Sea, cleft from shore to shore so that not a drop of water touched their feet.

So much of the Seder was to do with remembering. Rachel prepared the *maror*, the bitter horseradish that made those who ate it remember the bitterness of the lives of the children of Israel as they worked as slaves, building the pyramids. Hannah mixed the cinnamon and apple and raisins for the sweet *haroseth,* the symbol of the mortar that was not there to help their building, and also to remind those who ate it that with God's vigilance, life was still sweet, however difficult it became.

Gabriel took out the boxes of *matzoh*, the unleavened bread, a reminder that the children of Israel had no time to let their bread rise on the day they left Egypt so hurriedly. He unwrapped the silver dish and polished it until it shone. Isaac found the white silk, silver-embroidered cloth into which he placed the three *matzoh*. He was happy and relaxed, the outburst of anger at Juno forgotten, when all of a sudden there was a cry from Hannah in the kitchen:

"Juno, down, it's not for you."

Hannah had been testing whether she had put enough salt in the chicken soup when Juno jumped up to look in the pot. Isaac burst into the kitchen, his voice full of thunder rising above Hannah's more gentle scolding: "Greedy Beast! How did you get in again? Get out at once!"

Juno recognized the well-known temper.

"Greedy Beast!" Isaac shouted again.

This time Juno took flight not into the garden but into the dining-room. She could not resist rubbing her long silky grey coat against the folds of the crisp white, starched double damask table cloth. But there was greater temptation. It was a plump, white cushion, specially positioned on Isaac's chair.

It was there so that Isaac could lean back in comfort; a comfort the children of Israel never felt during the days when they were slaves in Egypt: the comfort of a free man. Well, now Juno was going to be mistress not slave. She jumped and landed in the very centre of the cushion and arranged herself elegantly. She looked very beautiful and knew it.

Hannah and the children came in to see what Juno was doing. They laughed.

Isaac came in and bellowed: "Greedy Beast! How dare you!"

Juno never got used to Isaac's voice, however defiant she tried to be. But she was not going to give in gracefully. She ran out of the dining-room and succeeded in returning to the kitchen at such speed that she found herself alone, with just enough time to jump on to the worktop and seize a leg of chicken. Then she was off.

This time she went into the sitting-room, where

she was never allowed. There were too many lovely things to knock over, too many fine fabric-covered chairs on which to deposit her long silver hairs. Once more the temptation was too great. She jumped on to the cream linen sofa.

She was just about to bite into the delicious meat when Isaac came in and found her and screamed: "Greedy Beast! This time you have gone too far."

Even Juno thought he was right but she still managed an aggrieved cry as she jumped down and crawled for refuge underneath the sofa. In her panic she tore at the cloth and with one last defiant wail, clawed her way *inside* the sofa!

The defiant wail changed to a muffled and piteous mew.

Isaac, much as Juno irritated him, much as he had tried to teach her obedience, much as he had warned her of the consequences of her actions, could not let her be strangled by the coils of the metal springs and, with a mighty shout of "Greedy Beast!" and an even mightier heave, he turned the sofa upside down. No giant could have done so

well. Not waiting to catch his breath, gently, oh so gently, he uncoiled Juno while she lashed out with her claws.

Then he drew breath and banished her with the loudest "Greedy Beast!" ever heard in the Jacob household.

Juno dashed into the hall and out into the garden and vanished among the daffodils. She had the grace to leave the chicken behind her.

There was not a moment even to bathe his clawed hands, the preparations had to continue. But Isaac found time to praise Hannah for the lovely cooking, to reassure Rachel about having to read in her halting Hebrew the passage from the Haggadah reserved for the youngest child, beginning "Why is this night different from all other nights?" He rehearsed it with her, and then helped Gabriel find the special wine.

At last Isaac sat down to read the notes he had written so meticulously in his tiny handwriting on bits of paper, placed inside the Haggadah, ready for what he would say to his family and guests that night. He was the scholar and teacher, he would never rely on memory. Each year, he liked to think and talk freshly about what the Passover means in today's world. As always, he found solace from his worries in prayer to the God he would love and praise to his dying day.

Now everyone and everything was ready. The guests welcomed. Juno forgotten.

Hannah looked beautiful in a blue, silk crêpe dress as she lit the white candles in the silver candlesticks, and their light made her lovely face glow. Rachel wore her special Egyptian sandals with their collage of pyramids and palm trees. Gabriel, in his best trousers, looked so handsome.

Isaac had changed into his white shirt, dark suit and silk tie, his shoes polished even harder than usual. He wore the special white silk cap that marked out the holiness of the day. After all that shouting at Juno, he was letting others talk, and resting the wonderful voice that would tell the best of stories and sing the best of songs the night through, until the story of the miracle of Passover was told, and his most solemn religious duty at an end.

The Seder began, the breaking of the *matzoh*, the drinking of the cups of wine, the spilling of the drop of wine from the cup as each plague God sent to Egypt was recalled:

Blood, Frogs, Lice, Wild Beasts, Pestilence, Boils,
Hail, Locusts, Darkness, and the Death of the First Born.

Gabriel and Rachel shared the Children's Haggadah and took it in turns to pull the tabs of the special pictures that brought baby Moses out of the bulrushes and the Egyptian soldiers under the Red Sea. The family and guests sang the many songs of praise:

He brought us forth
from bondage to freedom
from sadness to gladness
from mourning to feasting
from darkness to great light
and from slavery to redemption.

And then in the hearts of everyone at the Seder table, young and old, but in Isaac Jacob's perhaps most brightly, burned the wish that Elijah would come that Seder Night to announce the Messiah and the coming of peace on earth for ever and

When the moment came to prepare for the coming of Elijah, Isaac sprang up with his quick, eager step and opened the door.

In walked Juno.

And Isaac Jacob, being the forgiving man he was, greeted her warmly with a phrase from a Passover psalm:

Shomer P'taim Adonai.
The Lord guardeth the simple.

THE
GOLDEN SHOES

Adèle Geras

"You remind me," my grandmother said to me one day when I had chosen to put on a pair of silver sandals, "of the story of the Wisest Man in Chelm."

"Where's Chelm?" I said. "And who was the wisest man? And why do I remind you of him?"

"Take the silver sandals off and put them away and I'll tell you."

I put the sandals back on the shelf, pulled the curtain carefully across, hiding the beautiful shoes, and went to sit beside my grandmother on the bed.

"Chelm," she said, "is a small town which, they say, is right in the middle of Poland. Or perhaps it's Hungary. Because it isn't a real place, because you can't find it on any map, that means you can put it anywhere you like."

I smiled. "It's a magic place. It's somewhere you've made up."

"Me? I couldn't make up such a place if I live to be a hundred and twenty," said my grandmother. "Always, for as long as I can remember, there have been stories told about the people of Chelm and believe me, there's nothing magic about them. On the contrary, every single person who ever lived in the town of Chelm was a fool."

"Not one clever person in the whole town?" I asked.

"Not one. Fools, dolts, idiots and simpletons, from the teacher to the butcher, from the carpenter to the baker. And not only them, their wives and children too. They were fools as well."

"Were they happy?"

"They were as happy and as unhappy as anyone else, I suppose, but they had their own ways of solving problems."

"Did they have a problem about shoes?"

"Not about shoes, not exactly. What happened, happened like this. One day, all the people of Chelm decided that there should be a Council of Wise Men to look after the day-to-day business of the town. Ten people were chosen to be the Council, and then those ten people chose the cleverest among them to be the Chief Sage."

"But were they really clever?" I asked.

"No, they were fools. Everyone in Chelm is a

fool, whether his name is Chief Sage or not. You must remember that."

"I will. What happened next?"

"The Council of Wise Men decided that the Chief Sage should wear a special pair of golden shoes whenever he walked about the town, so that everyone would recognize him and see that he *was* the Chief Sage and not just an ordinary citizen. The shoemaker made a beautiful pair of sparkling golden shoes, and the Chief Sage put them on at once and went walking about the town. Unfortunately, it had been raining the night before and the streets were deep in mud. The Chief Sage had hardly taken twenty steps before his beautiful shoes were covered in mud and not the tiniest speck of gold could be seen. 'This will never do,' he said to the Council of Wise Men. 'No one could see my gold shoes because of the mud. What is the solution to the problem?'

The Council of Wise Men sat up all night debating the matter, and by morning they had found the answer: the shoemaker would make a pair of ordinary brown boots, which the Chief Sage could slip on over his golden shoes, thus keeping the mud away from their glittering surface. Oh, the Council of Wise Men was delighted with this solution, and so was the Chief Sage, and he stepped out happily in his golden shoes with the brown leather boots on over the top. To his amazement, however, not one single citizen of Chelm recognized him while he was walking through the town.

'"No one recognized me!' he cried to the Council of Wise Men. 'They couldn't see the golden shoes because of the brown boots covering them up!'

'"Aah!' sighed the Council of Wise Men. 'How clever of you to have worked that out! It's not for nothing we elected you to be our Chief Sage!' They sighed again. 'But what is to be done?'

"One of the Council had a moment of inspiration. 'I know!' he cried. 'Let the shoemaker cut a pattern of small holes along the side of the brown boots, and right across the toes, and then the golden shoes will be visible through the holes!'

"Murmurs of 'Brilliant!' and 'Wonderful!' rippled round the Council Chamber. The brown boots were taken to the shoemaker and he punched a pattern of small, star-shaped holes all over the leather. The Chief Sage put them on as soon as they were ready, and set off for another walk around the town . . . but again the streets were muddy, and the mud came through the holes and hid the golden shoes.

"No one recognized the Chief Sage and everyone in the Council of Wise Men was in despair. They discussed the problem for many days and many nights, and at last arrived at a perfect solution. Now, if you go to Chelm and walk around, you will know at once who the wisest man in the whole town is. It's quite clear. He's the one who walks about with a pair of golden shoes on his hands, wearing them as though they were gloves!"

I laughed and said, "Tell me another story about Chelm. Are there any more stories?"

"There are many," said my grandmother. "I'll tell you another one another day."

TISHA BE'AV
IN PUDDLEWICK

Ruth Craft

Solly was five, Rachel was eight, and they were Jewish children who lived in the East End of London during the terrible war between England and Germany which raged all over Europe fifty years ago. Solly and Rachel's father was a soldier and he was away from England with the army. Their mother looked after the children and worked in a factory while they were at school. Nearly every night there was a bombing raid over the East End and all the families would hurry down to the air-raid shelters to be safe from the bombs. Streets, houses, parks and shops were often destroyed by the bombs but although the people were often frightened, hungry and homeless, they carried on their lives bravely and tried always to help each other.

One Sunday morning, after a terrible night of

bombing, Rachel and Solly were having their breakfast. Rachel liked making volcanoes out of her porridge. She would scoop it up into a pile like a mountain in the desert. When she had got the pile shaped exactly right she poured milk over the top.

"Look Solly!" she said. "There's the lava pouring down the side of the volcano!"

"Sticky old lumpy porridge!" said Solly. He hated porridge.

"When you are as old as I am," said Rachel grandly, "you'll know about volcanoes. You'll know about lots of things."

"What things? Anyway, you're not old," said Solly.

"Oh, things like the war and rations and why there aren't any sweets and why there's black stuff all over the windows and why Mum is always listening to the radio and why Daddy is away fighting and why I can't be a bridesmaid for Uncle Max until he gets home from the war and why ladies have spots," said Rachel.

"Mr Cohen the Fish Man's got a spot. He's not a lady," said Solly.

"It isn't a spot. It's just a big freckle. Anyway I bet you don't know that Mrs Cohen has got verryclose veins. It's because she has to stand all day in the fish shop, Mum says."

"What's verryclose veins?" asked Solly.

"Just something else you don't know about. Quick! Finish your porridge! Here comes Mum!" said Rachel.

Mrs Silverstein's pretty brown eyes were red and swollen and she looked sad and distressed but she smiled at her children.

"Making volancoes again Rachel? Good boy Solly for finishing your porridge. Come here darlings. I have to tell you something sad and serious. Come here. Sit close, Rachel. Come on my knee, Solly."

The children did as they were told. They felt anxious as their mother was usually so cheerful and they had only seen her cry a few times.

"Now listen," said their mother. "On the radio just now there was an important announcement from the Government. It said that the bombings were so bad that it was no longer safe for children to be in London and that they must be moved away from their homes and live in the country with families who would look after them."

"Does that mean me and Solly? Does that mean

you won't come with us? Does that mean we won't come back here?" Rachel's voice was shaky and she brushed away the tears with the back of her hand.

"It does mean you and Solly going away by yourselves. I will know where you are all the time and when the war is over and Daddy is back, we will all live together again as a family. I promise," said Mrs Silverstein.

"When? When am I going away with Rachel? What is the country?" asked Solly fearfully.

"Darling, you are going tomorrow with Rachel on the train and the country is a place with trees and green fields where people grow the food that we eat," said Mrs Silverstein hugging Solly close. "Try to be happy, darlings. Try to be happy."

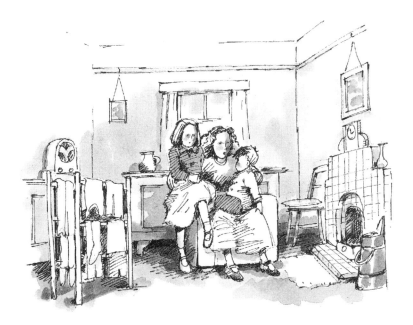

All day the family prepared for the journey and washed and ironed the few clothes the children had, and packed the suitcase. At suppertime Solly said, "What about Tisha Be'av? Will they have that in the country? And what about the peaches in the cupboard? You said we could all eat them on Tisha Be'av. You said we would try to plant a tree and that there would be a party!"

Mrs Silverstein reached up to the cupboard and brought the tin of peaches to the table. In those days tins of fruit were very expensive and many families could not afford to buy them. But people in other countries sent food to the people in London who were struggling every day with the bombings and the shortage of food in the shops. The Silverstein family had been given a parcel of food and in the parcel was a tin of peaches. It had a beautiful picture of some peaches growing on a tree under a bright blue sky and the words GOLDEN QUEEN PEACHES PRODUCE OF AUSTRALIA printed on the tin.

Solly stroked the picture with his finger.

"I bet they are the best peaches in the world," said Rachel.

"We will pack them in your suitcase," said Mrs Silverstein. "You can eat them on Tisha Be'av. I'll give you a note for the lady who will be looking after you."

The next morning at Waterloo Station Rachel,

Solly and their mother waited with hundreds of children for the special train that would take them to the country. Rachel and Solly held their mother's hand tightly. They each wore a little label on their coats which gave their name and address. Solly cried loudly and his mother picked him up to cuddle him. He held on tightly to the gold Star of

David that she wore around her neck and she whispered to him softly, "It won't be for too long, Solly. It won't be for very long." Rachel tried to comfort her brother as well.

"This horrible old war will be over soon Solly. And I'll look after you. I know all about the country and I'll show you all about the sheep and the pigs

and the cows. I've seen them in books," she said. "And they have kangaroos in the country. I know that for a fact," she added, but her voice was trembling and she could not stop her eyes filling with tears.

"There's my brave Rachel," said her mother. "I know you will look after Solly but you take trouble to look after yourself as well. It's time to get on the train, my darlings. Time to go now."

There was noise and confusion as the children left their mother. They joined the hundreds of other children who were all feeling sad, lost and alone as they climbed aboard the long train that was to take them to their new homes in the country. Rachel and Solly sat by the window. First they watched as the train chugged through the city of London. They saw many buildings which had been destroyed in the bombings and streets full of bricks and rubble but gradually the view changed and there were fewer houses and streets. Instead they began to see fields and trees and then they travelled over a long bridge with a silvery river sparkling in the sunshine below.

"This is a lovely country," said Solly.

"That river is the Amazon river," said Rachel. "But there are no crocodiles, I know that for a fact."

It was teatime before they reached Puddlewick station. The people of the little town were farming people and they had all agreed to take the children from London into their homes and look after them until the war was over.

Solly and Rachel waited on the platform with some other children. A lady who was helping with the arrangements for the children came towards them.

"Solomon Silverstein? Rachel Silverstein?" she said kindly. "Come this way."

Solly and Rachel felt very shy.

"Tell her to call me Solly," said Solly.

"Miss," said Rachel, "could you call my brother Solly? He always gets hiccups if you call him Solomon. Thank you."

"Of course, Solly," said the lady with a smile. She took the children's suitcase and led them towards an elderly couple. The man was very tall and broad and the lady was little and sprightly. She held on to the lead of a big Labrador dog. The lady spoke to them and they both smiled at Solly and Rachel.

"This is Mr and Mrs Briggs," said the lady. "And they are going to take you to their home."

Rachel and Solly looked at the dog. They weren't at all sure that they liked dogs. They had never had one in the family.

Mrs Briggs saw they were nervous.

"He'll not hurt you. He's as soft as butter. Soft as good Devon butter, that is. His name's Harry. Give him a pat. He'll like that."

Rachel and Solly each gave Harry a tiny pat.

"Now let's get you home for your tea," said Mr Briggs.

When Solly and Rachel went to bed that night their heads were full of pictures and sounds of the countryside: the wind rustling the early leaves on the trees; the little brook by the farmhouse gate where Mrs Briggs said there were fish and frogs; the crusty loaf of bread and jam and butter they had for their tea; the hens and the noisy old rooster in the yard, and Harry the dog chasing his tail on the back lawn.

"She was kind about the peaches, wasn't she Solly?" said Rachel quietly.

"She said she had never met Jewish people before," whispered Solly.

"Yes, but she said God bless you when you told her the peaches were for a special day," said Rachel.

Rachel and Solly missed their mother. They talked about her every night as they lay in bed. They had been with Mr and Mrs Briggs for some days when Tisha Be'av arrived. The day was made even more special for them because they had a long letter from their mother who said she was well and that she missed them and loved them.

Mr Briggs said they could have a picnic under the big elm tree on the hill behind the house.

"So, Rachel," said Mr Briggs as he ate his sandwiches and sipped a glass of cider, "what is this special day – this – how do ye say it?"

"Tisha Be'av," said Rachel. "Well, a long time ago Jewish people were farmers like you but then they were forced to leave their farms and to live in places called ghettos, but they have always wanted to go back to the country and grow food like you do. One day the Jews will leave the horrible ghettos and poor cities and go back to Israel and be farmers again. Israel is a faraway country quite near the Amazon."

"So Rachel and I are Jews and we eat fruit today like the Produce of Australia peaches and we sit under a big tree," said Solly.

"If we were at home we would go to synagogue and plant a tree but it wouldn't be very safe for the tree in London because of the bombings."

"Reckon it should be safe for anybody to plant a tree," said Mrs Briggs. "I'll try to find you a little sapling and you can plant it here in Puddlewick. Reckon this terrible war will be over soon and you'll be able to plant a tree where you like, in peace. But the one you plant here will remind us of you when you've gone."

"Plenty of good old trees around here. Been here fifty or sixty years some of 'em . . . you both take a good old look at 'em and say your prayer or whatever it is you do and God bless you both," said Mr Briggs as he began to clear away the picnic things. Harry stayed behind.

Rachel and Solly stayed on the top of the hill under the tree and played leap-frog in the soft grass. The old elm tree was very big and its trunk was huge. Harry chased flies.

"I bet I can get my arms right round the tree's trunk," said Rachel and she wrapped her arms around the tree and stretched. But her fingers wouldn't meet no matter how hard she stretched.

"I'll join up with you!" said Solly and went round to the other side of the tree and held Rachel's hands. Sure enough, their arms encircled the tree like a strong little rope and they both laughed in the Puddlewick sunshine.

SOMEONE WILL GET RICH

Leila Berg

Old Mrs Taylor was sitting outside her house. Her son Solly always put a chair out for her every morning on the front doorstep, so that she could hear people passing by, and have the sun on her face. Mrs Taylor was blind.

She heard Benny coming and she called out to him, "Is that you, Benny love? Did you take Joey for a nice walk?"

Benny had never stopped to wonder how Mrs Taylor knew everything that was going on, or who was passing by. But just for a second, he wondered if Mrs Taylor, who could hear everything because she couldn't see, had heard the pram with Joey in it going down Fern Street all on its own. And had she heard the man bringing the pram back – the man who was just as strange as the pram disappearing was strange?

He went across the road to her. "I took him down the hill," he said. "And his mammy gave me this." He took the gold stopper off a little bottle and put it under Mrs Taylor's nose.

She was startled at the lovely smell that came out. "What is it, Benny love? Is it scent?"

"Mm," he said, nodding. "Roses." And he tried to take it away from her nose to put the stopper on again, but she clutched hold of his hand, the hand that was holding the bottle, and took deep breaths.

"No, you mustn't, you mustn't!" he cried, distressed. "You're breathing it all up!"

But Mrs Taylor held tight to his hand, the hand with the bottle in it, and she breathed, and all she said was "Oh Benny love, oh Benny love!"

Benny was worried and puzzled. "It isn't fair," he said. "You're taking it all. And it's mine."

She let him take the bottle away from her then, and he put the stopper on to shut in what was left, but she still held his hand and beat it up and down on her lap. "Oh Benny," she said, "I can't ever see roses. Won't you let me smell the roses? You can see them and smell them too, the way they grow."

"I've never seen roses," said Benny. "Where are roses? What are roses like?"

But Mrs Taylor just shook her head. "I don't know, Benny, I don't know. But one day, you'll see roses. One day you'll see them. You're a good boy and a strong boy, and you'll work hard and have a nice wife and go to live in a beautiful house with roses growing in the garden, and peacocks maybe."

"I've seen a peacock," said Benny. "There's one at Boggart Hole Clough. We went there on a Sunday. It was a very long ride on three trams. And there was a peacock there, and we waited all day, and we drank pop while we waited, and then he spread his tail."

"I know," sighed Mrs Taylor. "My Solly has seen peacocks too."

"Why aren't there peacocks everywhere," said Benny, "instead of just pigeons?"

"It's God's will," said Mrs Taylor, sighing again. "Will you let me smell your roses again, Benny love?"

Benny undid the stopper once more, and put the bottle under her nose. But he did it unwillingly. She could feel his unwillingness, and she took only a very quick sniff and then pushed it away. "Go, Benny," she said. "Go, and keep well."

Benny stood up, relieved and glad to go. But now that she had given him back the bottle, he wanted her to have it again. He stood uncertain.

"What is it?" she asked.

"You can keep the roses," he said at last.

He was going to say more, but she grabbed hold of him and hugged him so hard against her enormous apron that he could scarcely breathe. He managed to gasp out, "But you must give me something in exchange. It's a sort of magic, to get a shoebox, for the nut games. I have to go on giving things and getting different things back, until in the end I get a shoebox."

"But, Benny," she said, "I haven't got a shoebox."

"That doesn't matter," he said. "The magic'll give me a shoe-box when it's time. You just have to give me *something*."

"I must sit on the step till Solly comes home," she said. "But you go into the kitchen, and see what you can find."

So Benny went into the clean tidy kitchen, that Solly cleaned every morning before he went to work, and he looked. He looked on shelves, in cupboards, in drawers, on window ledges. "I think it's too tidy in here for me to find anything," he called out to Mrs Taylor.

"Solly's good," she said. "He keeps it tidy so that I can find everything I want. If it isn't tidy, how can I find anything with my hands only?"

"Never mind," said Benny. "I'll go on looking." So he looked again, in drawers and cupboards, in boxes, on shelves and ledges. Every now and then, Mrs Taylor, sitting on the doorstep, smelling the bottle of roses, would put the stopper back so that the smell wouldn't be wasted while she talked, and call to him, "Well, Benny, have you found something?" And he would call back, "No, Mrs Taylor, nothing at all."

At last she called to him, "Come here, Benny, I've something here for you. I've just remembered." And when he came, out of the pocket of her enormous apron, she took a letter in an envelope.

Benny thought she was going to ask him to read it for her. He hoped she wasn't, because he wasn't very good at reading spidery foreign handwriting. Ever since he started to go to school, people were always asking him to read letters for them or to write letters for them, because most of the grown-ups in Fern Street couldn't read or write themselves.

And although Benny felt proud that he could do something for them that they couldn't manage for themselves, all the same the writing was very hard to read and sometimes the spelling was quite different from the school readers.

Benny started to wrinkle his forehead in a worried way. But instead of asking him to read the letter, Mrs Taylor took the paper out very carefully, put it in her pocket, and held out the envelope.

He took it very doubtfully. She could feel he was not very eager, so she said excitedly, "See! It's the stamp!"

Benny looked at the stamp. To him it looked like any other stamp. Of course the picture was different, and the words on it weren't English words, but he couldn't see anything special about it.

"It's a *new* stamp," said Mrs Taylor proudly. "And

if you keep it on that envelope, then it'll make you a rich man."

"How will it do that?" said Benny.

"If you keep it on that envelope, and if it has the date on the envelope, then it'll show that this is the very first time a stamp with that picture on it has ever been used on an envelope." She paused for breath.

"I don't know anything about that," said Benny undecidedly.

"Me, I don't know either," Mrs Taylor said, shrugging her shoulders. "But my Solly knows. My Solly told me. 'You keep that, Momma,' he said to me, 'and one day you'll be a rich woman with diamonds maybe.' But how long can I wait to be rich? You're a young boy. You can wait a long time. Take it."

Benny considered. It was a very complicated business. "But it isn't for me," he began. "I won't be *able* to keep it. I have to exchange it. I told you."

"All *right*!" said Mrs Taylor, shrugging again. "All *right*! Exchange it! Let Joey Samuel get rich! Let Eli Jacobs get rich! You'll get rich with your shoebox! Should I worry who gets rich?"

So Benny thanked her, and took the envelope. As he went down the steps, she called to him anxiously, "Don't be a fool, Benny, and take it off the envelope. The stamp without the envelope is nothing. The stamp on the envelope is something wonderful. My Solly told me."

"I won't forget," said Benny. And he left Mrs Taylor, with her enormous apron stretched over her wide knees, smelling . . . smelling . . . smelling the roses.

THE POWER
OF LIGHT

Isaac Bashevis Singer

In World War II, when the Nazis had bombed and burned the Warsaw ghetto, in one of the ruins a boy and a girl were hiding – David, fourteen years old, and Rebecca, thirteen.

It was winter and bitter cold outside. For weeks Rebecca had not left the dark, partially-collapsed cellar that was their hiding-place, but every few days David would go out to search for food. In the bombing all the stores had been destroyed, and David sometimes found stale bread, cans of preserved food, or whatever else had been buried. Making his way through the ruins was dangerous. Sometimes bricks and mortar would fall down, and he could easily lose his way. But if he and Rebecca did not want to die from hunger, he had to take the risks.

That day was one of the coldest. Rebecca sat on the ground wrapped in all the garments she

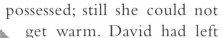

possessed; still she could not get warm. David had left many hours before, and Rebecca listened in the darkness for the sound of his return, knowing that if he did not come back, nothing remained to her but death.

Suddenly she heard heavy breathing and the sound of a bundle being dropped. David had made his way home. Rebecca could not help but cry, "David!"

"Rebecca!"

In the darkness they embraced and kissed. Then David said, "Rebecca, I found a treasure."

"What kind of treasure?"

"Cheese, potatoes, dried mushrooms, and a package of candy – and I have another surprise for you."

"What surprise?"

"Later."

Both were too hungry for long talk. Ravenously they ate the frozen potatoes, the mushrooms, and part of the cheese. They each had one piece of candy. Then Rebecca asked, "What is it now, day or night?"

"I think night has fallen," David replied. He had a wristwatch and kept track of day and night and also of the days of the week and the month. After a while Rebecca asked again, "What is the surprise?"

"Rebecca, today is the first day of Chanukah, and I found a candle and some matches."

"Chanukah tonight?"

"Yes."

"Oh, my God!"

"I am going to bless the Chanukah candle," David said.

He lit a match and there was light. For the first time Rebecca saw their hiding-place – bricks, pipes, and the uneven ground. He lighted the candle. Rebecca blinked her eyes. For the first time in weeks she saw David. His hair was matted, and his face streaked with dirt, but his eyes shone with joy.

In spite of the starvation and persecution David had grown taller, and he seemed older than his age and manly. Young as both of them were, they had decided to marry if they could manage to escape from war-ridden Warsaw. As a token of their engagement, David had given Rebecca a shining penny he found in his pocket on the day when the building where both of them lived was bombed.

Now David pronounced the benediction over the Chanukah candle, and Rebecca said, "Amen." They had both lost their families, and they had good reason to be angry with God for sending them so many afflictions, but the light of the Chanukah candle brought peace into their souls. That glimmer of light, surrounded by so many shadows, seemed to say without words: Evil has not yet taken complete dominion. A spark of hope is still left.

For weeks David and Rebecca had pondered about escaping from Warsaw. But how? The ghetto was watched by the Nazis day and night. Each step was dangerous. Rebecca kept delaying their departure. It would be easier in the summer, she often said, but David knew that in their predicament they had little chance of lasting until then. Somewhere in the forest there were young men and women called partisans who fought the Nazi invaders. David wanted to reach them. Now, by the light of the Chanukah candle, Rebecca suddenly felt renewed courage. She said, "David, let's leave."

"When?"

"When you think it's the right time," she answered.

"The right time is now," David said. "On Chanukah the moon never shines. I have a plan."

For a long while David explained to Rebecca

the details of his plan. It was more than risky. The Nazis had enclosed the ghetto with barbed-wire and posted guards armed with machineguns on the surrounding roofs. At night searchlights lit up all possible exits from the destroyed ghetto. But in his wanderings through the ruins, David had found an opening to a sewer which he thought might lead to the other side. David told Rebecca that their chances to remain alive were slim. They could drown in the dirty water or freeze to death. Also the sewers were full of hungry rats. But Rebecca consented to take the risks; to remain in the cellar for the winter would mean certain death.

When the Chanukah light began to sputter and flicker before going out, David and Rebecca gathered their few belongings. She packed the remaining food in a kerchief, and David took a piece of lead pipe for a weapon, his matches and a compass.

In moments of great danger people become unusually courageous. David and Rebecca were soon on their way through the ruins. They came to passages so narrow, they had to crawl on hands and knees. But the food they had eaten, and the joy the Chanukah candle had awakened in them, gave them the courage to continue. After some time David found the entrance to the sewer. Luckily the sewage had frozen, and it seemed that the rats had left because of the extreme cold. From time to

time David and Rebecca stopped to rest and to listen. Then David lit a match and looked at the compass. After a while they crawled on, slowly and carefully. Suddenly they stopped in their tracks. From above they could hear the ringing of a trolley car. They had reached the other side of the ghetto. All they needed now was to find a way to get out of the sewer and to leave the city as quickly as possible.

Many miracles seemed to happen that Chanukah night. Because the Nazis were afraid of enemy planes, they had ordered a complete blackout. Because of the bitter cold, there were fewer Gestapo guards. Despite the curfew,

David and Rebecca managed to leave the sewer and to steal out of the city without being caught. At dawn they reached a forest where they were able to rest and have a bite to eat.

Even though the partisans were not very far from Warsaw, it took David and Rebecca a week to reach them. They walked at night and hid during the day – sometimes in ditches and sometimes in barns. The peasants stealthily helped the partisans and those who were running away from the Nazis. From time to time David and Rebecca got a piece of bread, a few potatoes, a radish, or whatever the peasants could spare. In one village they encountered a Jewish partisan who had come to get food for his group. He belonged to the *Haganah*, an organization that sent men from Israel to rescue Jewish refugees from the Nazis in occupied Poland. This young man brought David and Rebecca to the other partisans who roamed the forest. It was the last day of Chanukah, and that evening the partisans lit eight candles. Some of them played dreidel on the stump of an oak tree, while others kept watch.

From the day David and Rebecca met the partisans, their life became like a tale in a story-book. They joined more and more refugees who all had but one desire – to settle in the land of Israel. They did not travel by train or bus. They walked. They slept in stables, in burnt-out houses, and wherever they could hide from the enemy. To reach their destination, they had to cross Czechoslovakia, Hungary and Yugoslavia. Somewhere at the seashore in Yugoslavia, in the middle of the night, a small boat manned by a crew of the *Haganah* waited for them, and all the refugees with their meagre belongings were packed into it. This all happened silently and in great secrecy because the Nazis occupied Yugoslavia.

But their dangers were far from over. Even though it was spring, the sea was stormy, and the boat was too small for such a long trip. Nazi planes spied the boat and tried to sink it with bombs, and Nazi submarines were lurking in the depths. There was nothing the refugees could do besides pray to God, and this time God seemed to have heard their prayers because they managed to land safely.

The Jews of Israel greeted them with a love that made them forget their suffering. They were the first refugees who had reached the Holy Land, and they were offered all the help and comfort that could be given. David and Rebecca found relatives in Israel who accepted them with open arms, and although they had become quite emaciated, they were basically healthy and recovered quickly. After some rest they were sent to a special school where foreigners were taught modern Hebrew. Then David was able to enter the academy of engineering in Haifa, and Rebecca, who excelled in languages and literature, studied in Tel Aviv — but they always met on weekends. When Rebecca was eighteen, she and David were married. They found a small house with a garden in Ramat Gan, a suburb of Tel Aviv.

I know all this because David and Rebecca told me their story on a Chanukah evening in their house in Ramat Gan about eight years later. The Chanukah candles were burning, and Rebecca was frying potato pancakes for all of us. David and I were playing dreidel with their little son Menahem Eliezer, and David told me that this large wooden dreidel was the same one the partisans had played with on that Chanukah evening in the forest in Poland. Rebecca said to me, "If it had not been for that Chanukah candle David brought to our hiding-place, we wouldn't be sitting here today. That small light awakened in us a hope and strength we didn't know we possessed. We'll give the dreidel to Menahem Eliezer when he is old enough to understand what we went through and how miraculously we were saved."

Acknowledgements

The publisher would like to thank the copyright holders for permission to reproduce the following copyright material:

Lynne Reid Banks: The author and Watson, Little Ltd for "Batata" by Lynne Reid Banks. Copyright © Lynne Reid Banks 1996. **Leila Berg**: Hodder & Stoughton for "Someone Will Get Rich" from *A Box for Benny* by Leila Berg. Copyright © Leila Berg 1958. **Ruth Craft**: The author for "Tisha Be'av in Puddlewick" by Ruth Craft. Copyright © Ruth Craft 1996. **Phyllis Rose Eisenberg**: The author for "A Mensch is Someone Special" by Phyllis Rose Eisenberg. Copyright © Phyllis Rose Eisenberg 1982. **Deborah Freeman**: The author for "Elijah at the Door" by Deborah Freeman. Copyright © Deborah Freeman 1996. **Sheila Front**: Scholastic Children's Books for "Jacob and the Noisy Children" by Sheila Front, André Deutsch 1991. Copyright © Sheila Front 1991. **Adèle Geras**: Laura Cecil Literary Agency for "The Golden Shoes" from *My Grandmother's Stories* by Adèle Geras, Heinemann 1990. Copyright © Adèle Geras 1990. **Barbara Diamond Goldin**: Penguin USA Inc. for "Just Enough is Plenty" by Barbara Diamond Goldin. Copyright © Barbara Diamond Goldin. **Marilyn Hirsh**: The Estate of Marilyn Hirsh for "Captain Jiri and Rabbi Jacob" by Marilyn Hirsh. Copyright © Marilyn Hirsh. **Tamar Hodes**: The author for "Special Fridays" by Tamar Hodes. Copyright © Tamar Hodes 1996. **Miriam Hodgson**: The author for "The Open Door" by Miriam Hodgson. Copyright © Miriam Hodgson 1996. **Judith Kerr**: HarperCollins Publishers for the extract from *When Hitler Stole Pink Rabbit* by Judith Kerr, Collins 1971. Copyright © Judith Kerr 1971. **Michael Rosen**: Peters, Fraser & Dunlop Group Ltd for "The Judgement" from *The Golem of Prague* by Michael Rosen, André Deutsch Ltd 1990. Copyright © Michael Rosen 1990. **Isaac Bashevis Singer**: Lescher & Lescher Ltd for "The Cat Who Thought She Was a Dog and the Dog Who Thought He Was a Cat" from *Naftali the Storyteller and His Horse Sus* by Isaac Bashevis Singer. Copyright © Isaac Bashevis Singer 1976. A.M. Heath & Co. Ltd for "The Power of Light" from *The Power of Light – Eight Stories for Hanukkah* by Isaac Bashevis Singer. Copyright © Isaac Bashevis Singer 1980.

Every effort has been made to obtain permission to reproduce copyright material but there may be cases where we have been unable to trace a copyright holder. The publisher will be happy to correct any omissions in future printings.